50

7/90

The Spanish Inn

Jean Louis Bergonzo

THE
SPANISH
INN

Translated by Helen R. Lane

Grove Press, Inc.
New York

I It seems to me, though I couldn't swear to it, that I was told to wait here. For the moment I might say, with the proud certainty that I am not mistaken, that my life is a corridor (unfolds in a). For I am, actually, in a corridor. I have no intention (my eyes are still too clouded over) of constructing a fine image, with literary pretensions and all that, on this theme (one fine image, by the way, was all I ever possessed: a square of rough cardboard, the postwar kind, awarded by the school authorities when I was in grade school for a reason that at present escapes me, for I was messy, a dolt, and a chatterbox—doubtless so as not to discourage me; it represented, I think, a green boat on an indigo sea, and it also had, it seems to me, a yellow lighthouse on the end of a jetty rising up in the left-hand corner of the drawing, unless it was a bridge over a river with a boat; I don't remember now); I am, therefore, unable to collect enough substance in words to reach the perfection of the image, that is to say, to compose a whole, bordered on each of its sides by a colorless band or a zone of silence, and in itself, I mean within this framework, possessed of a subtle, balanced, and—why not?— learnedly academic meaning. Nothing about my situation lends itself to literary artifice anyway, nor to fine painting either, since I am standing in my pajamas in a corridor which is perfectly bare: seeing neither a boat nor a lighthouse, nor even a bridge or a river, and limited by the fact that it is necessary for me at this moment to reduce all inner discourse to the simplicity of this sort of schema, which now seems perfectly definitive to me. I wish nonetheless to explain this necessity.

5

It must be recognized that the least poetic complacency with regard to my situation would immediately plunge me into a serious and dangerous illusion and, I must say, this is not the moment to daydream, for my safety here is more than threatened. Though this corridor (or hall, or perhaps vestibule) is striking because it is so bare, a bareness that up until now has been only fleetingly glimpsed by me, for I have been absorbed in contemplating a red waxed hexagon neatly inscribed between my two feet shod in raffia, there is nonetheless nothing that prevents me, you will agree, from imagining that it has an entry and an exit, both represented by a door (that can close all by itself if need be, or automatically, with a noise like a suppressed fart or with the creaking of a spring that needs oiling), unless this door or these doors is closed by a bolt that may have been slid shut, simple logic constraining me to set aside at least three hypotheses: 1) the corridor has only one end, 2) it has no end at all, 3) it is neither opened (nor closed) by any door. Even though this beginning of a proof runs the risk of appearing hasty, a laudable concern for exactitude, together with a resolution comparable to that of the Cartesian traveler lost in the forest who, having once thought over the route or direction to take, makes the firm decision not to depart from it until he reaches the edge of the forest (if he can find it, what with a pond rosy and shimmering in the twilight, and in the distance a transparent steeple erected in the valley, and noises, let's say soft moos and bleats, cock-a-doodle-doos and the angelus) causes me to decide to retain, even though the three hypotheses enumerated above are capable of seducing a mind that is adventurous or enamored of the absurd or the fantastic, to retain, I say, only my first postulate, which, even though it may be reassuring, still presents very thorny prob-

6

lems. But to tell the truth, I do not feel, I no longer feel, the need to come back to it, I don't want to come back into this corridor, let's say neither for the present, since I am already in it, nor once I get out of it, if I do get out of it, which also naturally poses many a problem, at least two of which cause me to be inclined to curb, if not to reject, every impulse aimed at such an eventuality. Outside of the effort necessary to find a way out, it is, in fact, painful for me to imagine, or to try to predict, what I shall find beyond, let's say, the door whose existence is accepted as a postulate. I can, of course, attempt to review the possibilities, in no order of preference naturally, which would imply a calculation, a reflection on any part that would be incompatible with the sincerity of my discourse, namely: another corridor, a stairway, the sea, the void (or nothing), latrines, the bridge of a passenger liner, the parlor of a whorehou.., a classroom, a middle-class residence, a sewer, the street, and here the game is too easy. Although I feel no particular repulsion for any one of these places, and though I would even be quite willing to see myself in them (in each one of them) after leaving this corridor, I nonetheless can not conceal from myself the fact that in a certain proportion of cases, let's say three out of five, I am constrained to pose the second problem, which at this juncture is a problem of esthetics or perhaps simply of modesty. For I believe I have already pointed out the precariousness of the way I am dressed (a precariousness reinforced, as it were, by the near-failure of the elastic which is holding my pants up, and the unbelievable looseness of the buttons on my pajama jacket), which does not offset the total absence of more intimate underthings. I wouldn't mind if it were the middle-class residence or the toilets, or even the sea, all of these being places where it would be

7

possible for me, not only not to be noticed, but also to shuck off my clothes if I feel like it, without offending anybody or violating the normal order of things. I confess, however, that I would feel better in a suit (with a shirt, a tie, silk socks, and good shoes of fine black leather), even if it were ready-made. I can't see myself, may I say, in pajamas in a sewer, for instance, any more than I can in a suit; that's why it's better to set aside the hypothesis that our antechamber has a sewer at the exit. In any case I feel no aversion to these pajamas; I don't know where they came from, but they look so much like pajamas I remember having worn that they might be mistaken for them, and perhaps they're the same ones (I hardly ever wear them, since most of the time I sleep in all my clothes, or else bare-ass naked, depending), that is to say, they're made of a soft, loose, striped material (one wide blue stripe, then a white one —or rather cream-colored, and quite dirty—which is almost as wide, with a brown line, a blue one, a brown one in it, then another wide blue stripe, and so on), which material, more or less fuzzy in the beginning, or with a raised nap, has now worn down to one or two thousand fine grayish fibers, and fits me the way all my pajamas did, namely not at all, and by this I mean to suggest that the legs are too short, and the sea.. too wide, while the slit in the front, which serves as a fly, goes down much farther than what would normally be necessary, which thereby causes . . . I do not bring this matter up to create a diversion. And I can not, and do not wish to, hide or ignore what is happening in the meantime. It began as a sort of rustle. A far-off monotonous, intermittent noise made the terra-cotta squares or hexagons vibrate imperceptibly. Breaking the strict parallelism of my feet which were partly the object of my meditation, I placed the heels closer together, while the tips of the toes, by contrast, spread apart, which (leaving out of consideration the doubtful esthetics of two hairy legs jutting out from the trumpet-shaped orifice of a pair of ordinary pajamas, and the rest following as a matter of course, that is to say, from bottom to top, butto.. tucked in, stomach sucked in, shoulders free and back straight, head high) constitutes a position, at once relaxed and ready for action, highly recommended by dancing masters, or a basic, fundamental, position. And then I began to look ahead of me, that is to say, toward the head of the corridor but not the end of it, for whether this extremity was the end or the beginning of the corridor did not depend on the way I was oriented to it; I mean, for example, that I had perhaps entered it by the exit. What confirms my certainty that this is true is the fact that the noise that I spoke of, which now, moreover, was growing louder (horses' hooves hammering on dry earth) was coming straight from the rather hazy place that I had turned my eyes toward, and I have always granted others a logic superior in rigor to my own, in consequence of which I could not conceive that those who were making this noise (granting that it was produced, and not the cause of itself, or imagined by me) could be entering otherwise than by the entrance, unless what to me was the exit was to others the entrance, but in that case beware. As for this noise, which in the beginning was only an intermittent buzzing, it was growing louder, as I have said; it was becoming, as it were, more compact as the intervals of silence grew shorter, which amounts to saying that the intervals of noise were in the end getting closer and closer together, dangerously so, I might say, so much so that I had begun to expect an auditory telescoping that to all intents and purposes was inevitable. I shall add that the corresponding vibration (a muffled and relatively prolonged shaking at the base of my heels) had the same pattern. The better to persuade myself that it was not at all a question of an illusion on my part (a pure reverie, or a proprioceptive phenomenon—an arterial pulse, for example, more and more violently localized), I embarked upon a series of oscillations from front to back, that is to say, I shifted the weight of my body now to the front, onto my tiptoes, now to the rear (my first position) onto my heels, and I can state that each time, or better put, regardless of the zone of contact, the floor sent back the same message to me. At the same time I observed that the rather distant design representing the end of the corridor had a tendency to change structure (it became proteiform) in the exact rhythm of this uniformly accelerated respiration (this is what I call the vibration), undergoing, so to speak, spasmodic contractions that made it pass through the following forms: 1) Concentrated brevity, 2) filiform and apparently indefinite protraction (I am all the more hard put to define these forms in geometric terms in that, as far as I can remember, this corridor did not answer, in my mind, the formal requirements of a corridor, as might have been expected—I mean by that, that far from appearing to me to be, according to the laws of perspective, something like a pyramidal funnel, that is to say, formed by four more-or-less isosceles triangles meeting at the top, it instead took on the form of a parallelepiped seen without perspective, so that, had it not been for my undoubtedly longitudinal rocking back and forth, I might have believed that I was living in, or on, or against, a perfectly flat and vertical universe in the shape of a rectangle). It was only by assuring myself that I could execute my gymnastic exercise three paces forward (or backward as well) that I was in a position

10

to see through this deceptive geometry. For had the contrary been true, I might truly have been a figure, standing there just as I was, in a flat image representing a guy in pajamas against a uniform background. Convinced of the functional thickness of my being, I began to pay more attention to the auditory-sensory-visual shaking that I have doubtless alluded to before, and I made a heartfelt attempt to make my own oscillations correspond to the rhythm of these shakes. Now it must be made clear that these shakes were not limited to affecting the base of my heels or the tip of my toes, or let's simply say the soles of my feet; they also proceeded upward, faithfully following the rhythm of the successive waves, probably along my legs—although I felt nothing in this part of my person—so that they had an effect principally on the top of my thighs and the groin and then the base of my neck, while my ears registered the ringing, in unison with the distant metamorphosis of the corridor. But at this moment it (the corridor) seemed darker to me (doubtless night was falling) or else I closed my eyes. Or then again, perhaps, heavy, tepid fogs had blurred my sight, if not my senses. Then again, perhaps, I mean to say, it was a sort of corridor, let's say an Eastern one, the air of which seemed tepid, heavy, and perfumed. Its exotic hangings, drenched with the perfume in question (the odor of armpits and a moist sex organ), were doubtless the garments of the woman who then appeared to me to be a soft, warm giantess, or else the folds of her trembling flesh, contorted with pain perhaps, and Lucile was breathing more and more rapidly, just as the rapidity of my gasps was increasing, and I too, what else was there to do, deaf, blind, for all my senses, as well as myself, were probably projected to the tip of my coc.., that is to say that I was, myself, localized precisely in my peni..,

11

struggling against asphyxia or drowning only so as to space out my oscillations, for I believe that at each instant I was on the verge of completely abandoning myself to being buried. And from Lucile's depths surged fleecy waves, heavier and heavier and closer and closer together, but I can't remember whether these waves imitated the cadence of my rocking back and forth, or whether it was I who forced myself to respect the afore-mentioned cadence; in any case the whole unfolded strictly in phase, so that anyone who could have said who or what would have had to have all his wits about him. At the same time, moreover, the muscles of my thighs grew warm and heavy, and I knew that I couldn't hold back, that is to say, avoid the telescoping (im-possible to arrest or turn this train of mad waves aside) for I was forbidden, so to speak, to slow down, and moreover what way was there to slow down a movement that did not depend on me—I don't say that just because it is probable that Lucile would not have liked me to temper, to temporize, or to slave away with more modulation, but because this sort of human see-saw moved like a pendulum in accordance with a kind of cosmic respiration that it would have been abnormal to have tried to smother. And it was while this sort of monody in double time (always double time, but each measure being in a different rhythm from the preceding one, according to the law: $T = x$, where x tends toward zero) was going on that we were disturbed, it was while I was wholly concentrated, as I said, in my peck.. and thrusting and drawing back, or better put, by turns letting myself fall and raising myself up in this narrow and trembling corridor, traversed by moist waves, I mean in the sex organ, since it must be called by its name, of Lucile (she too must be given a name), that events altogether exterior to and independent of us

12

came to trouble our (fornication?). I should explain
that although these events were independent of us, they
were nonetheless predictable. But we had obviously conducted ourselves with rare insouciance, and this insouciance was as rare as the love, I dare say, that it
sprang from—we had thrown ourselves without the
shadow of a hesitation onto the shadow of an opportunity. I proved to be all the more imprudent and blame-
worthy in that—had I so desired—I could have been
perfectly conscious of (have taken into consideration)
the noise that kept coming closer and closer, a noise
made up of a muffled stamping (dark color) and of
snatches of loud conversation (lighter spots), but so
many mental images, along with that of danger, could
not decently fit into what was, after all, quite a small
number of cubic centimeters of flesh convulsed by burning and palpitating nerves, I mean the end of my peni...
To tell the truth, I was neither conscious nor uncon-
scious of it, but I hoped, and like to imagine, that Lucile
found herself in the same state of mind, that we would
arrive at the famous telescoping, or at time t, such that
$x = o$, that is to say, at the moment when my oscilla-
tion would appear to a (virtual) lateral observer, not as
a series of successive positions, but as the image of a
fixed triangle with the apex at the bottom, set, in a
manner of speaking, in a vibrant immobility, granting
that this possible observer would be able to disregard
the agitation liable to be engendered in him by the
spectacle that Lucile and I would be giving him, to
master his senses and to consider the question only
from a geometric angle, with a cold, intellectual cast of
mind. We then doubtless wanted to hasten the advent of
my triumph (or of my defeat) and our haste was
directly proportional to the imminence of the intrusion
that would not fail to take place—and thus the single-

phase rhythm that I have spoken of. But within myself I had definitely made up my mind to notice nothing, reserving for myself the possibility of remaining sheltered should it be necessary (as it was presently), in Lucile's lower belly, nice and warm and wet, but in that case also immobile and quiet, and as if I were all curled up in a ball (fetal, as it were), demanding only to prolong this stay forever. The voices, however, drew closer, and with them what were perhaps footfalls, and I noticed that the individuals organizing this uproar seemed to be bringing with them what was probably complex and heavy, or at any rate noisy, equipment, but I welcomed these impressions without the question of what they were intending to do with these tools ever crossing my mind. I noticed, furthermore, that the number of voices, and of footfalls, was increasing, so that soon they turned into no more than a uniform, thunderous sort of rumbling, which came very close to reproducing all the frequencies the human ear can hear (from low to high, for example, the rumble of the heavy equipment, the footfalls, the voices, the creaking of the light equipment); so that as a result at the very end I suddenly realized that everything was gathering in upon itself (a crowd bunched up at a door) as if to pile up in one last wave, and the voices became expectant and threatening, and it was then that the body of the woman raised up with a cry that resounded down the whole length of its fibers, and by conduction, or contagion, in mine (she had pressed her thighs together forcibly and lifted her cun.., so as to drive me out in one last gasp) in the same moment that all perceptible space was filled with a crowd of people, a crowd screaming: whor.., bastar.., which literally unfurled while I was still panting from the effort I had expended to remain, whatever the cost, right where I was, with the regrettable

14

spectacle of my pollution, moreover, visible to all eyes, and feeling quite frustrated, their arrival having prevented me from..., but hoping nonetheless that my pajamas would not betray the use they had been intended for and would preserve part of my dignity. It was a veritable charge that descended on me, something equivalent to a herd of bison, such as almost everybody has had the chance to see, either in reality, or at the movies, or on television (or has been able to imagine). They were not absolutely enraged, as might have been expected, but on the contrary obviously full of composure, advancing very quickly but in orderly fashion (and I saw their frozen masks and their leaden eyes), like male nurses, or soldiers; I even saw their rifles and their threats, the whole borne by a thick thunder at the heart of which one could sometimes make out sharp, abrupt, clacking noises, like a false note in a mediocre performance, answered almost immediately by the sound of a metallic echo. Though I can not help feeling guilty, I do not believe that I committed an error, since I don't even know whether it was I who went to meet them or whether it was they who . . . I was forced to realize that Lucile had betrayed me, and that the entire national guard had suddenly sprung up, so to speak, from between her thighs. I nonetheless wish to state, with all the strength I can still muster, that I do not hold any feeling of ill will toward her, even though at the time I was convinced that she had treacherously cleared the way for them, as it were (N.B.: This is doubtless the way that Spain was born and died in a day, betrayed by its very love). But I was unable to think any of these thoughts in the middle of this rumbling. I heaved a long and grievous sigh, that of a man prostrated, intentionally modulating it in as bestial a register as possible, vaguely hoping that I was giving a reply, however lame it might be, to the other voice that was screaming around me and filling the place with its cataclysmic presence, an enormous, compact mechanism. The uproar was so violent that it seemed as if it had no intention of ceasing until one and all were duly stretched out full length on the ground, or huddled up, or curled up rather, to complete the picture, with thick blood (dark red, with a few soft, opaque bubbles, then with the help of time, curds or clots, like darker islands) leaking from their split eardrums. Rumblings, whistles (steam or compressed air), the whole crescendo, on top of the vision that I then had of the tunnel, soon to be strewn with corpses (I have mentioned these blown-up bodies), made my sigh turn into a scream such as one does not often have the chance to emit (out of modesty, dignity, or lack of space), which I must at once say passed completely unnoticed. It is true that despite the notable quantity of decibels that I contributed to the disturbance around me, it is true, as I was saying, that I tried as hard as I could, perhaps out of a sort of modesty, to conceal the origin of this sort of contribution by keeping my mouth more or less closed. Although my humble vocalizing, launched out of bravado, as it were, was not destined to last more than a few seconds (ten in all), the production of this nasal flight of sound came close to exhausting me, for the energy that I put into containing and channeling the vibrant air that I was exhaling through my nose and imperceptibly open mouth, in order, I repeat, that the source of the cry not be detectable, in opposition to the natural force of this cry (a movement and its contrary), made me flutter my glottis painfully, at what must have been the rate of ten to fifteen vibrations per second, and the evaluation of this frequency, whose rhythm spread progressively, moreover, to all the muscles of my pharynx, allowed me to predict an irresistible fit of coughing sooner or later. I nonetheless succeeded, by skillfully regulating the volume of the sound, in surmounting this possible lapse, and put an end to my scream, by a fully voluntary decision, only when the train itself stopped, it too having calmed down, contenting itself with echoing my own breathlessness by letting out invisible curls of compressed air and hiccuping rhythmically to recharge its pumps, while I got into the next to the last car, no longer trying to suppress my cough. But this business of shooting waterfalls (the fit of coughing), in which it's easier going up than it is coming down, soon wearied me, and to allay it I inhaled big mouthfuls of the smell of warm, wet briefcases that never fails to pervade the subway trains at this hour of the morning. I knew, without even trying to consult the wrist watches of other people (I have no confidence in mine, although it keeps excellent time) that I was already a bit late, but I avoided thinking about it, knowing that the time to run would come soon enough when I got to my stop. All my thoughts, moreover, were concentrated on the most important event in my existence at this moment, namely Cécile's leaving, which had long been conceivable and even predictable, and was doubtless now an established fact. Long hours of indifference and sarcasm had, as it happened, finally made me aware that she was escaping from us little by little, probably freezing me within herself into an image of myself that was perhaps false but in any case was certainly justified by my attitude. Example: I come home at four o'clock and give her a quick peck (but anything else would surprise her and fail to come up to her expectations, because for her I am what she expects me to be) because I'm all out of breath (we live on the eighth floor and there's no elevator) and therefore haven't the strength, and am not in the mood, to give her any sort of embrace. A few minutes, though, are enough for me to get my wind and my energy back, that is to say, to get my breath and get over the irritation I always feel after I've worked for several hours, and I would then be in a position to mollify her, by talking to her, by giving her proofs of my attachment to her, but it's too late, for Cécile has already turned her back, has shut herself up in her bad mood, once again chewing over the complaints she has about me. From then until it's time for dinner, which she prepares in exasperation, I sometimes sleep, which doesn't soothe her irritation, though this act in itself is as peaceable as can be, and sometimes I try to work: I correct a theme (sometimes only half of one), get up, walk around for a few steps, or else circle the whole apartment, once, twice, making sure to drag my heels, like a man who's terribly weary—I'd like to have her feel sorry for me, but she feels too sorry for herself because of me to feel sorry for me. I go into the kitchen. I always see her from the back (even in bed). I look at her blond hair ("my hair's in a dreadful mess"), the delicate nape of her neck, her tan shoulders ("the color of my skin is terrible"), her little as.. nicely molded by her skirt, her tan legs (the same skin tone again), the fragility of her shoes or her mules, the whole undulating rapidly from top to bottom, simply caused by the movement of an arm stirring mayonnaise, for example (I detest mayonnaise). I know that she won't say anything to me while I'm watching her this way, although she is not unaware that I'm there behind her. From that moment on I avoid saying anything, for the vocabulary of our conjugal effusions has long been one that has shrunk considerably.

("What's the matter with you tonight?"—"Nothing.")

Invariably. Useless then to. I go back to my desk even

more slowly than I came to it, and then flop down in front of it. Always the same. Sick and tired. Doesn't love me any more. Not worth the trouble any more. She doesn't. I'll go away. But also, what. I'm. What a. To think that. Over with now. Over with. Yes indeed. Ended. No longer possible. Can't last. Wait till, till, till. She'll see that. No, but. No, but all joking aside. We'll really find out what. There you are. No, Godda.. And bam. And bing, and bang. There you are.

("You coming to eat?"—"Yes (my love), GOOD LORD.")

And a silent meal. Feels contempt for me. What, but I do everything I can, I never, etc. It would doubtless have been necessary to say and do so many things for this not to have happened, something like a thousand or two thousand times in the course of two (or three) years of marriage. It would have been necessary, of course, but what things? So that she didn't leave, this morning perhaps, or else last night. Without taking anything with her, certainly. My existence already seemed empty to me; today it is even more so. That could happen then, though I might have believed that I had touched bottom long since. Emptiness. Be careful of words. I want to be suspicious of them, and of their syntax. I want to tell only what's happened, what's happened to me. And that morning, for it was indeed morning, I began to find that a number of disagreeable things had already piled up. Cécile's leaving, for example, was obviously very significant. It means that the absence of her flesh will deprive me, that we won't spend a vacation in Spain this year (which I don't) and not only because Spain has ceased to be a country one vacations in, ever since—suffering Spain. Will we ever get to Spain? It's already Spain here, it's still Spain. I wanted to see it immediately. I left the subway car and its smells. I knew that I was late and that Monsieur Rotenstein (Rôtennstaïnn) was not about to forgive me for it. But I stepped out onto the platform and went to sit down on a bench, placing myself approximately in the center of the bottom of a poster (all the posters are in gaudy colors; we shall not mention this again). So: my briefcase resting on my knees, held fast on one side by my elbows, my hands supporting my head and forming a screen before my eyes at the same time, my palms and the joints of my fingers folded at right angles so as to shade my eyes. It was not exactly the void that I was contemplating at that moment, but rather a uniform background (the brownish crust that constitutes the subway platform). I arranged myself so that this uniformity was complete, that is to say, I oriented my gaze in such a way that the boundaries of my universe constituted by my hands did not include, for example, the line formed by the edge of the platform, an overly garish bit of paper, or (especially) any person whatsoever. But soon I was no longer able to preserve this horizon of absence, for the gates to the platform had just opened again, and I heard heels hammering on the cement. I then applied myself to the task of watching people pass by, or rather not them, but the bottom of their legs, and their shoes, wondering now and then if I were not, indeed, in the subway in Barcelona or Madrid (two-color shoes and baggy pants). I saw them pass through my field of vision, at first one by one, coming in and going out, then in denser and denser groups, and soon from both directions at once. This hesitant and confused choreography had something depressing about it (calling exhaustion to mind) and above all something worrisome, for the uncertainty of the figures in it betrayed the obscure desire to form a hostile and threatening half-circle around me. This could be surmised without its being necessary to consult each of the faces corresponding respectively to each of the pairs of shoes. (I forbade myself, moreover, to do so, as I have explained above.) If such a thing didn't happen, if the menace died a-borning, the truth of the matter is that they were more in a hurry to catch the subway than they were to fight a counterrevolution, and that doubtless conformed with the imperious desire of an authority which preferred to see its soldiers work in a factory or in offices (those of the radio broadcasting network, for example). And doubtless there was some regret, some shameful nostalgia in the gesture the members of the phalanx made, turning slowly away from me and scraping the floor (namely: I saw feet, or rather shoes, dark, hard, tough shoes, make a quarter-turn, or even in some cases a half-turn), turning their backs to me, as it were, taking to their heels, and going off to post themselves in front of the longitudinal ditch in which the roaring subway cars were running, perhaps leaning out dangerously from time to time to see if a train was coming, with something in their attitude also that doubtless recalled (legs stiff and a far-off look in their eyes) their former militance, that they had just renounced by no longer being interested in my person. The militia aboard the express leaving for the front of mental action drew away, and its odors and noises raveled at the edges. Then there were still other troops, other trains. I took one of the latter. Not without first having suppressed a terrible desire: that of leaning over a sleeping bum (colorless and syphilitic shoes, pleated pants, an immense overcoat he was all huddled up in, the whole surmounted by headgear in the shape of a cap; from the front, nothing, he's all down inside his coat, feet, hands, and skull alike, and perhaps he is even physically absent from this cast-off clothing), a desire, I was saying, to slyly lean over him and shout at him as loudly as possible the name of the station, RÉAUMUR–

21

SÉBASTOPOL, for example. I would then perhaps have had the pleasure of seeing him spring up out of his rags, terrified and, in a word, fearsome, either frightened or delighted at being thus called back to life. For that's what life is, Réaumur–Sébastopol, Roux and Combaluzier, she and I, you and I, and above all else the danger of dying. But I remembered that the town had long since been taken and lost again, and I left him there, a dead body among other dead bodies, at the foot of the walls. So I left with the others, making, in short, a more than honorable retreat toward another defeat. My escape begins here. I was already in flight before the battle, not having yet decided. But I didn't find this out till later. When I finally came out into the fresh air, the electric clock at the intersection told me that I had managed to be as late as I had ever been in my whole career: twenty-three minutes. I then began to run, swinging my briefcase with an irregular motion, while a veritable cataclysm took place inside my clothes, which were, in fact, not exactly intended for this sort of exercise, and consequently refused to conform to all my movements, which did not make the efforts I was making any easier, and heavy vapors accumulated under my raincoat. Yet I continued to run, despite the fact that I was becoming more and more uncomfortable. This conduct, furthermore, was perfectly inconsistent: I was running because I was late, but I was forgetting that in order to explain myself and not have my being late held against me I was going to need breath and composure. Arriving as soon as possible so as to minimize the bad impression my carelessness would make was one thing, but being capable of giving my lapse from punctuality an elegant, and therefore convincing, explanation in the presence of authorities who would doubtless be mesmerized by my air of assurance, and therefore favorably disposed as

22

one naturally is toward a man who knows how to assert himself, was something else again, and doubtless preferable. But my haste prevented me from confronting these two necessities lucidly, and thus when I got to the door of the school I found myself dripping with sweat, my clothes sticking to my skin in big patches, and a fifty-pound weight rising and falling in my chest, alternately lifting me up and letting me fall back down again, like an elevator out of control. I rang the bell briskly, and the spiteful door took its time as it opened, increasing my feeling that everything was going wrong. The glass door of the concierge (Monsieur Janus), the vestibule, the inner courtyard (a square of grass, three starved-looking flowers, to our dead), a stairway which plunges into darkness, leading to the vast schoolyard of glass and metal, the work of an engineer named Eiffel—all this I saw through a veil of fog and tears, for I was literally drowning, and I do believe that on that day I was not far from having exhausted the eighty per cent that this liquid represents (so they say). Standing in the center of the schoolyard, not far from a puddle of water, the remainder of rains that the canopy dreamed up once upon a time by Gustave Eiffel could no longer hold off, were the vice-principal (pronounced Rotanstin, and not Rôtennstaïn) and the assistant principals, who were doubtless, as far as one could judge by their faces, mulling over some grave problem (I was even afraid that it was about me and my being late). I changed the trajectory of my run toward the stairway that leads to the upper floors so as to pass close by this stern triangular group. The noise of my heels on the cement floor caused them to turn around, each of them rotating the number of degrees that corresponded to his previous position in relation to me. I then slowed to a stop, saying:

"Monsieur

Oh (he said) these parents of pupils who monopolize teachers to the point that they make them miss the bell
It (I said) was not parents of pupils that made me late but the simple fact that my watch stopped and
Monsieur (he said) monsieur monsieur don't act like a schoolboy
I (I said) am not acting like a schoolboy but I
Come (he said) come come you're giving us an excuse that is not worthy of you the excuse that
But (I said) I'm not
Yes (he said) you are yes you are yes you are
However (I said) I
I (he said) know I know I know"

Thus: "However—You don't—I—You don't—I—You don't—I you."

(Go on (he said) go on go on find your pupils.)

I hesitated for a moment, seeing by the one same expression on the faces of the assistant principals that they disapproved of me, for they had been careful to nod their heads when the vice-principal had gravely declared: Come come monsieur. Night. Everywhere inside it was night. With no stars, for this night did not come from the sky, but rather from the stained-glass window, too dirty to let the daylight through, from the ceilings, the walls, and the floors. I thus plunged into these thicknesses, the nape of my neck still burning from the glance of the authorities, nonetheless feigning the resoluteness, or even the insouciance, of someone who knows perfectly well where he is going and why, my shoulders back, my head high, with a firm grip on the handle of my briefcase in my moist hand (in my left hand, as my right fiddled with the bits of fuzz lining the bottom of my raincoat pocket)—hunting for my class, hunting the noises and shouts of my class (the herd: forty, stamp-

ing. He's not here—yes he is, I tell you, he—shut u..—
no he's not—this morning I—shut your trap, we're going
to be—dam.., here he is). But I heard no such thing.
Nothing except the noise of my footsteps cutting into
the almost silent humming that large buildings have.
The iron stairways intermingled with the passageways,
shooting up and crossing each other in bizarre scrolls
that I ran up, faster and faster, feverishly as it were,
probably out of the fear of being later still—which I
unquestionably was now, for I had just passed by the
same place for the third time while the bits of fuzz at
the bottom of my pocket, by dint of my having kneaded
them, had formed, or been agglomerated into, a single
irregular ball mixed with shreds of tobacco, which I
extricated from my raincoat by pulling slightly on a few
threads sticking out of the seams, and which I threw
down over the railing of a passageway in the direction
of the three skulls* of the vice-principal and the assistant principals, running all the while and looking like
some heavy and hesitant insect wandering over the
walls, and from time to time glancing furtively at the
skulls arranged in a triangle in the middle of the con-
crete rectangle. It is not beyond the range of possibility
that they might have looked at me, in spite of or because
of the noisy and agitated efforts I was exerting to go on

---

* Naturally the object in question hit none of them, for the
following reasons, each one of them, moreover, being sufficient:
1) The subject's fear of calling attention to himself, since he
already found himself in a bad situation and was not on the job
as yet; 2) this gesture was indubitably hesitant, for it constituted
an obvious lack of respect; 3) even if the act of throwing it had
been more decisive and more powerful the lightness of the pro-
jectile, plus the resistance of the air, would have inevitably de-
flected the initial trajectory assigned it.—*Author's note.*

25

my way unperceived, although I never once saw their eyes turned toward me. In any case, they showed no outward sign which might have given me some idea of what opinion of my conduct they were entertaining at that moment, as my more or less spiral journey continued beyond the bounds of all decorum. Curiously enough, although I was perfectly conscious of the indecent lengths to which I was going, by robbing, as Monsieur Rotenstein had probably not failed to point out, the administration of a few pennies, so to speak, and despite my scrupulous intention of finding my way again, it seemed to me that part of my will had taken its leave of me, abandoning me in these mad traceries, as if I were intoxicated by the circumvolutions that I kept on performing, and also intoxicated, in a manner of speaking, by my panic. I was searching very actively, let there be no mistake about that, but I lacked a real desire to find. And so I turned and circled, describing vast ellipses (in the half-light of the schoolyard) whose silhouettes, gathered together in a triangle on the asphalt, formed one of the centers. At the end of a space of time that must have been quite long, since it had allowed me to perform a rather large number of my revolutions, I glimpsed, or rather it seemed to me that I perceived, at the end of one of the main passageways, the silhouette of the principal, looking stiff and elegant, and perfectly discernible although haloed with fog (but perhaps the fog was already concealed in my eyes). My path would inevitably cross his if I failed to change direction immediately, and with the presentiment that in my embarrassment I would be extremely hard put to it to furnish an acceptable explanation for my behavior, I took a sharp turn to the left when I was fifty paces away from him, taking advantage of a probably little-used stairway that was right there. I went down, came back up, turned left or right several times, depending, and suddenly I found myself in front of him (the principal) standing in my path like an icy reproach. I could thus see his face—a face of marble (this was the first time that I had had a chance to contemplate it from so close up)—and his person seemed to me to be much less elegant than it appeared to be from a distance, and somehow even repulsive, for I am in a position to state that his suit was shabby and shiny in the places that got the most wear, that he was wearing thick, yellow, very worn shoes, that his completely ordinary face had several disagreeable things about it, namely: two warts, one on the left nostril, the other on the chin, this latter displaying a thin plume made up of a few sorry curly hairs, eyebrows that were bushy and irregularly (badly) shaped and, finally, a tic which drew the left corner of his mouth up toward his ear (on the same side) at the rate of one twitch every fifteen seconds or so (which would have allowed me to estimate how many times this nervous movement had taken place during the time he'd been watching me running). Naturally I halted two paces away from him, imitating the way he stood there motionless, for I had already realized from his grave look that he had decided to speak to me, and there was no way for me not to devote all my attention to him without giving the impression that I was disrespectful. I stood there expectantly for a very long moment (but my expectations were not deceived)—the principal, on his part, was in no hurry and was enjoying the right to silence that was his by virtue of the authority invested in him, or else the little speech that he was planning to present me with wasn't quite ready yet; then finally, between two twitches of his mouth:

"So (he said) then monsieur you don't
Monsieur (I said) I offer you my respectful

That's (he said) fine monsieur fine fine but I (he added) find you will permit me to find it strange that you

Monsieur (I said) is most kind to deign to inquire into my case that is why I am going to try to explain my

Do you (he interrupted) mean by that that I would perhaps not be likely to understand what you intend to

I (I protested) didn't mean that at all but monsieur

Very (he said) well very well very well I'm listening

It (I said) so happens that I somehow can't find my class

Well (he said) that's certainly strange you (he said consulting his watch) have theoretically at least been on duty for exactly thirty-four minutes and some forty seconds at the moment that I pronounce the word seconds you are at the same time standing here in front of me in this passageway far from your classroom but what are your pupils doing you have absolutely no idea who knows they may actually be sacking or destroying school property or committing murder or perhaps even the worst sort of sexual depravity

(We exchanged a look of fright at the mention of these forty-some adolescents giving themselves over to some monstrous phallic orgy in the corridors of the building.)

and (he went on) all this forces me to conclude that a serious negligence on your part

I (I said) assure you monsieur that

I (he conceded) do not doubt your good faith but the fact

Certainly (I said) appearances are against me but monsieur I beg you to take into consideration the fact that I ask only to find my class and

That is for (he said) tunate that is fortunate that is fortunate but nonetheless that is the least that could be expected of you that is why I cordially invite you to

Of (I said) course monsieur and I

That (he said) 's fine let's call it over and done with where are your pupils

That (I said) 's exactly what I

What (he said) you don't

I (I said)

What (he said drily) room

Room (I said after having glanced at the notebook that I had just taken out of the left inside pocket of my suit coat or jacket)

851 A-I on the fifth floor

I (he interrupted) am sorry but this room doesn't exist or rather it no longer exists any more than the fourth floor does and it's been that way for two weeks already

However (I said) it seems to me that I taught in this room several times during these last two weeks

That (he said) 's impossible

I (I said) assure you

No (he said) monsieur I value you may be sure your sincerity but in the present instance I

Monsieur (I said) I

No (he said vehemently) you haven't you couldn't have taught in a room that doesn't exist or else you are pulling people's legs or else you lack a sense of logic or else you have lost your sense of reality or else you are a liar which in this case as in the three others scarcely honors you will agree the profession I shall even go so far as to say the priesthood that you claim to be a member of

But (I said in confusion)

Don't (he said) say another word you are guilty in any case haven't you read the bulletins

Certainly (I said) I always read them

You (he said) aggravate your case by lying again on top of your other faults for I shall apprise you since you

29

didn't know it the bulletin that I circulated among the personnel the Monday before last stated clearly that from that date forward the numbering of the classrooms was going to be changed to conform to a more logical, more sensible system conforming to the layout of the buildings that I consider myself honored to have set up thus breaking with a tradition of assigning numbers whose sole advantage, and a meager one at that, was that everybody was familiar with it but with the enormous disadvantage of favoring one of the basest human inclinations I mean to say this refusal to rethink to redo which characterizes all our habits now it is my opinion that habit itself even though it appears a priori to be convenient must give way to logic and that is why I wrote and circulated a bulletin the fruit of long and judicious perfectly judicious reflections drawn up in this form for I flatter myself that I know the contents of it by heart unlike certain teachers who are placed under my jurisdiction for their greatest good since I am thus in a position to refresh their memory and call them to order once again Considering (he recited half-closing his eyes) that the distinctive numbering of the classrooms of our establishment must be adapted to the requirements of the categories of the mind that we profess to exercise and cause to progress for the greatest possible good of our pupils as well as for the disposition of the various locations a new system has been instituted and replaces the old one beginning today first point the old system of numbering the floors is hereby abolished and the fourth floor disappears nominally but not materially becoming the third as a consequence of the disappearance of the first floor which up to now has wrongly been considered that which becomes or better put again becomes as it should always have been the mezzanine thus the basement remains the basement lettered B the ground floor remains the ground floor lettered GF the first floor becomes the mezzanine lettered M the second becomes the first numbered I-F the third becomes the second numbered II-F the fourth becomes the third numbered III-F second point the first figure in the number of the classroom is determined by their position in relation to magnetic north beginning with the classrooms situated on the north side they will be numbered north 1 south 2 east 3 west 4 the numbers that follow can be found according to the position the classrooms occupy starting from my office which is in short the spiritual and material center of the establishment and proceeding clockwise fourth and final point moreover and in addition in order to avoid any sort of error the classroom can be located lastly according to the name of the teachers teaching in them by utilizing the initial of their surnames and proceeding by alphabetical order the forty-third classroom situated in progressive and ascending order on the mezzanine on the west side used for classes by teachers Alpha Beta and Gamma in alphabetical order will receive the following designation M—4/43 A-B-G that is why (he concluded opening his eyes again) the classroom that you maintain that you are searching for no longer exists and you should know that but alas (tic)* there are always some people who"

I was confused by so much perspicacity, lucidity, and intellectual rigor on the part of a person of such exalted station, and that is why I stood there a few moments without being able to speak.

"It is (I finally said) indeed the simplest and easiest

---

* Let us regret that despite the concern for precision that the subject claims to have, this is the first and only mention of the appearance of the nervous tic affecting the face of the P. Moreover, the place in which he points it out shows that he gave in to the temptation of making a disastrous pun.—*Author's note.*

way of determining the location of classrooms and I permit myself the liberty monsieur of offering you my respectful congratulations on the reform that you have conceived which at last puts an end to the bad habits that we have certainly contracted by remaining attached out of laziness to a worn-out system badly adapted to the progress that we must not only follow but also anticipate insofar as our modest means permit and I believe that in the present case thanks to the resourcefulness of your mind such is in fact the case and that you thereby furnish us with an admirable example of

Very (he said) well very well very well

I (I added hurriedly) am going to my classroom immediately I offer you monsieur my respectful salutations and beg you to please excuse my carelessness a carelessness for which you have penalized me only by being kind enough though I do not deserve such kindness to furnish me the explanation for a true and proper situation which there is no excuse for my not having been acquainted with but rest assured monsieur that it will not happen again and I shall make every effort to conform to the most remarkable example that you have offered us in this school you see I am conforming to it already and am going immediately to take over my class permitting myself to take leave of you with all due respect"

His eyebrows hadn't moved one bit during this flood of words (I wish to point this out particularly, for his tic—and I hope I will be forgiven for not mentioning it before, though there was in fact no reason or motive for not doing so—did not affect his eyebrows), but the tic produced itself at a rate that had increased noticeably, doubtless in active, joyous response to my laudatory circumlocutions. Profiting from this sort of advantage I made a move as if to go around him and past him, happy, when all is said and done, to be able to get away from him so easily, but he stopped me with a wave of the hand.

"Granting (he said) that you find your classroom which as you will recognize I have the authority to ask you to do you still won't be in a position to resume your teaching duties for your students won't be there

Ah (I said) I suppose that you have also changed the assignment of students to the various classrooms and I already congratulate myself on

Not (he said) at all not at all not at all that would be a superfluous useless and even harmful reform one of those redundant complications that every honest and lucid mind is obliged to avoid like the plague and I am surprised that you have the frightening audacity to maintain that you are following my example by coming out with such enormously inept

Quite (I said) so quite so what was I thinking of but would you please be so enormously kind as to

You (he said) ought not to be ignorant of the fact that after a delay of fifteen minutes students no longer wait for their teacher in front of the door of the classroom but rather are directed to study halls under the supervision of a day-school teacher so that is where you must go look for them

Really (I said) there is no excuse for my

Quite (he said) true quite true quite true you are

But (I said) what room must I proceed to for the number and disposition of the study halls in the building still escapes me and I don't know whether the system envisaged by you includes the study halls as well

It (he said learnedly) does it does but to be certain that you will take up your duties this morning I shall take you there myself

33

I (I apologized) am truly distressed at making you waste
your precious time doing so it is really too kind of you
and I would not want to
Allow me to tell you (he said) that nothing precious is
wasted in our little world when an intelligent person is
in charge of it and that if I take the trouble to guide
you there it is on the contrary so as to avoid an addi-
tional waste of time and correct the reprehensible insouciance that you display with regard to the most ele-
mentary rules of punctuality, promptness, and fidelity
to regulations therefore (he wound up) follow me"
I fell into step with him confidently and gratefully,
thoroughly overcome by an awkward embarrassment
and confusion, and yet the lesson hadn't had the desired
effect, for to tell the truth, and I acknowledge the fact
to my great shame, I did not make the slightest attempt
to remember the itinerary for future occasions, for I was
quite satisfied to walk behind him and observe the rigid
nape of his neck and his somewhat round-shouldered
back. Obviously he knew by heart each of the possible
itineraries in this world whose master he was, and nego-
tiated the corridors, the passageways, and the stairways
of this labyrinth with remarkable skill. We climbed immense dismantled iron ladders, passed through endless
vestibules, crossed vast lost lecture halls, and as we went
along the thought occurred to me that demolition work
must have gone on here recently, for as a rule I wouldn't
have been able to see the inside of them, as was now the
case. In short, these lecture halls, most of them empty,
made of iron and wood, did not seem to have any walls,
and what should have been the ceiling disappeared
somewhere up overhead. He for his part did not display
the slightest sign of amazement when we passed by the
classroom where madame or mademoiselle (I'd never
dared to ask her whether she was married) Lucile, the

34

Spanish teacher, was holding her class, a woman who was very nice to look at and doubtless to smell, a desirable woman—whereas I for my part gave a sudden start* at the sight of this class whose nature I have indicated above, for it was really unheard of (or at least appeared so to me). Forty brown heads (or thereabouts) were turned toward the teacher's desk, each student (I suppose that that is what they were) having on the floor at his side a briefcase or a sea bag or a traveling case, and all of them were looking at the blackboard, inscribed, as they say, with the following, written in Spanish:

> Es tan alta la nave
> De mi marina
> Qué ningún marinero
> Se determina
> Se determina

That was all harmless enough. But I was astonished because madame (or mademoiselle) Cécile, let's say just plain Cécile, was naked (yes, absolutely naked), thus displaying to all eyes, between the chair and blackboard, the coppery sheen of her skin and the somewhat heavy fullness of her figure, as she calmly sat on her varnished chair, her legs carelessly (no, nonchalantly) crossed, and one elbow delicately leaning on her desk. It even seemed to me that she recognized me and addressed me, prettily pushing her blond hair out of her face, a greeting that seemed to me to be tender and cordial, but so discreet that I couldn't swear to it. At that

---

* This memory is exaggerated. At the most it was a slight, somewhat weary, astonishment, of the sort that one feels when one undergoes an emotion that has been experienced too often. —*Author's note.*

moment I would have liked to be one of her forty students, or to prolong the way our eyes met, though it was becoming almost painful to me, but it is customary not to bother a colleague during a lesson and I was supposed, moreover, to be following the principal. I therefore hurried to catch up with him, though—I say it sincerely—not without bitter regrets. It was as I went by other deserted lecture halls that I promised myself that I would fight to the last of my strength, even though it cost me my life, to find Lucile, this woman (my) who had been foolishly lost through an irreparable mistake that was my fault alone, for I knew absolutely that I was the only one who could trace back all the virtues of Old Spain to their source within her. Thus, two paces away from her, from my lost Cécile, my lost Spain, an incalculable distance already separated us, and at the very moment that I should have been devoting all my time and all my strength to finding her again, to heal the tear in my heart (for this moving breath that overtook me as I watched, as I ceased watching Lucile was perhaps a tear, I mean a wound, let's say an emotional one), at that very moment, I say, I was obliged to walk behind the principal, a pompous, self-important old duffer for whom I was nothing, no, not even a man of learning, above all not that, nor even an unhappy * man, but only a faltering and disoriented element that must be hurriedly put on the right road again. We finally reached a tall swinging door, with dirty (or painted) glass at the top, and he halted there. I realized that it was the study hall where my students were, and as I

---

* Let there be no misunderstanding. Unhappiness is just a word here, as is pain. For Lucile (or Cécile) has very likely not yet deserted her conjugal domicile. This feeling is therefore purely potential.—*Author's note.*

questioned him (with my eyes), he nodded his head. I then put my hand on the copper handle, but he stopped me with a wave of his hand and lifted a finger to his ear (which I therefore began to observe though I didn't understand), looking at me gravely. One second, no, a fraction of a second later, the electric bell began to ring, a fearsomely strident sound that instantly filled the whole building so that neither of us (the principal and me) could hear what I was saying. He made no effort to answer me, satisfied merely to keep his eyes riveted on mine, his forefinger in the air, standing there motionless except for the tic which came over him four times during the forty-five seconds that the bell officially rings at the end of a class (or at the beginning of the next class). When there was silence again, his eyes blinked several times and he said to me:

That an hour had now gone past, that I had made my students lose an hour and stolen an hour's salary from the government, but that he would reserve the privilege of taking it out of my pay, that he hoped that this would not happen again, otherwise he would find it necessary to take measures against me that would be as painful for him as for me, and, finally, that I had five minutes to get to the room that I was to teach in the following hour.

Having said this, he disappeared without responding to my gesture of farewell (just a simple nod of my head). But instead of immediately searching out the classroom that I was to occupy, as he had so to speak enjoined me to do, I made up my mind to spend a few minutes in the teachers' room first and headed that way, laughing up my sleeve at the idea that the location of this room had no place in the logic of the principal's system, for the aforementioned teachers' room is located, and has always been located, above the third floor (the former fourth floor, though I couldn't care less), in the attic properly speaking, where it is, moreover, the only space that is in use. I was hoping to meet a few colleagues there, perhaps even (why not?) Cécile, and in any case I was counting on resting there for a moment and taking advantage of this brief leisure to get into my pigeonhole and see what mail I had. I came across this room very easily, having taken all the stairways that went up and having come out under the roof, where it turned out to be a simple matter for me to find the right door, unless the whole thing had happened by sheer chance. On first glance the room seemed to be deserted, and I nonchalantly flung my briefcase onto the long table in the center of the room, after which I started to unbutton the three buttons of my raincoat with a weary sigh. I was then extremely surprised when I noticed something that I had not been conscious of before. The demolition work must have gotten this far (and been left unfinished), for the ceiling had been removed, and the roof too, allowing one to see a sky that was cloudy and gray yet gave off a very bright light, and part of the walls, for the whole top third of them had likewise been torn down. Looking at them more closely, I saw that even their paint (cream-colored) had been removed and that they were bare now and built of old, badly joined boards. Even from where I was, that is to say, right under the open sky (had it not been for the table and the coat racks, one might have thought that one was on a sort of terrace), I could easily see outside the building, which allowed me to note that all the scaffoldings around me were likewise made of badly joined boards, but most of them still had a roof over them, for the most part made of nothing but corrugated sheet metal. It (I then thought) is curious that nobody has realized this state of affairs, and that it took a teacher in a public school who had a bad reputation with his superiors to first notice, when demolition work was being done in his school, that the top of the city is rotten, and that we are such miserable cowards we tolerate these enormous abuses. It was all the more revolting inasmuch as the majority of these shabby roofs had antennas (for television, I suppose), all of them gleaming, and luxurious even, which made for a very sorry contrast. Doubtless the government knew nothing about all this, and I promised myself that I would write a report about this some day, which would surely cause something of a scandal. I was even more furious when I tried to sit down. All the chairs had been removed, and one was doubtless supposed to infer from this that the teachers henceforth would be constrained to hold their meetings standing up. The sad thought crossed my mind that nothing was done to make life easier for us, even though we certainly needed rest, if not consideration. The sight of a person standing at the other end of the table, a presence that up to now had been felt but ignored, drew me out of my reflections. My eyes probed the fog that separated me from her, and I saw that it was the principal's secretary; this woman was known around the school for her unattractive looks (some people even spoke of her repulsive ugliness) and it was also rumored that she was a hot number, although I could not quite understand, looking at her, how and with whom she might prove to be so. So there she was, standing motionless at the other end of the table with a file of papers under her arm. At first I stood where I was, rocking back and forth from one foot to the other, hesitating. But common courtesy demanded that I greet her, and I knew that it would have been imprudent to get in bad with a creature who was said to have a great influence on the opinions the principal had about the behavior of his personnel inside the school. I even went so far as to ask myself whether this person had not deliberately set his secretary on my trail in order to observe my conduct and later tell what she had seen, to spy on me so as to make some sort of a report on me. That is why I resigned myself to bowing slightly as I looked in her direction, as a way of greeting her; once as a start, then several times more. Let's say four in all. She didn't budge an inch. I was disconcerted and upset, but I didn't let it show and walked resolutely over to her. Her look shifted slowly as I came around the table, what I mean is that she continued to look at me, and we found ourselves literally face to face because I had halted so close to her; myself in person, firmly planted on my two legs. Arrogant, even. I mean that that is the way I wish I had been. Her features didn't belie her reputation. Her face was worn and angular, and certainly very dirty, somewhat as if she had allowed the traces of years of lust to accumulate there without ever trying to erase them, even by just washing. As I tried to see what sort of file she had, I perceived that it had disappeared (doubtless I dreamed it), but above all I noticed in the same glance that she was dressed almost in rags, and her grayish skin peeked out through them in several places. I didn't know what to say. She gave me a toothless smile, as if to lead me on—but to what, for heaven's sake?—and I ardently wished that a colleague would come in so that his intrusion could help me get out of this unpleasant situation, for almost anybody in my shoes would have been embarrassed. But nothing happened, no, nothing, not even the bell announcing the beginning of another class, which would obviously have been the best reason for taking leave of this creature. Just as the insistent pounding of a little vein on my temple warned me that I was somewhat upset, I perceived that I had made a laughing-stock of myself, having drawn closer to her than would have been necessary for a simple good morning, or even a compliment just to be polite, and that the surface of her body, hidden by the rags, or whatever it was that I call rags, was even smaller than I had thought in the beginning. I could clearly see, without even trying to make it out, the roundness, that's right, the roundness of her shoulders which were very close, to tell the truth, to my mouth, and, I am still wondering why, her firm, full breasts (a bit lower down) that were warm too, and my face almost touched hers, in which her eyes were shining with a savage gleam. A burning heat came up from my lower belly, and we found ourselves actually coupled, without my having made the least gesture in this direction (I swear it). Arms (hers) moved about me, somewhat like snakes, and I kneaded her body feverishly. My pleasure was: immediate, brief, and dreadful, like lightning (I should like to have it again), invading me before I could even get an idea of where I was and what I was doing. She then gave a rather frightening sort of cry, throwing her head back, and I felt ice creeping over me. But she clung to me, unsatisfied, still seeking her pleasure around the frayed remains of mine. Getting the better of my terror and pain, I shoved her brutally toward the wall; she toppled silently over the sort of balustrade that it happened to form just there, and probably fell to her death in the depths of the building. This put an end to the dreadful ambiguity of my feelings. I hastened to hide my moist penis, wishing to shelter it from the cold that was quite noticeable at this altitude, buttoned up my fly with a trembling hand and straightened my

41

clothes a bit, then went to the exit as fast as I could, still feeling uncomfortably dressed for walking, it is true, and with a pain in my groin. Once in the corridor, I listened attentively. Not the slightest sound. (I was afraid that someone might have been alerted by the uproar which perhaps could have been heard from quite a distance away.) I went downstairs again, using the metal ladders that had replaced the stairways so as to allow access to the upper floors during the demolition work. At one moment I was obliged, if I didn't want to retrace my steps, to go through a classroom in which my colleague, Monsieur Heptaméron, a distinguished teacher of history, was teaching his students (whom I did not see, however, either because they were plunged in shadow, or because Heptaméron, whose absent-mindedness was well known, was perchance teaching in front of an empty classroom).

"When (he said) in eighteen hundred seventy France declared war on Prussia to get the point across that the French armies were ready for battle the Emperor Napoleon III was told boys that not a gaiter-button was missing does this mean boys that our soldiers had to fight against the enemy by projecting these tiny buttons with their thumb and forefinger not at all."

I went across the lecture hall as discreetly as possible, but neither he nor his students noticed me. Finally, as I continued downward, I went through several cellars and found myself in a dark and shabby little courtyard strewn with plaster dust, with blind walls so high that one could hardly make out the sky. Suddenly overcome with a great weariness, I sat down in a corner, put the collar of my raincoat up and carefully closed it over my neck, and little by little a gentle torpor stole over me. I thought of Lucile whom I had cheated on, and realized that she would have liked to leave. I felt miserable and

abandoned, quite ready to give up the battle I was wag-
ing in my life to earn a living, which did not prevent me
from losing her (or it) at every moment (Cécile, I mean
my life), so as to assure and to regain our happiness. It
was as I engaged in these reflections that I fell fast
asleep.

2 I don't know how long I slept. I love to sleep and never stint myself when it's a question of doing something I like to do. I woke up with my as.. bruised from the pieces of plaster I was sitting on and stiff all over. I was certain of one thing at least: that the sky must have been cleared of its February haze, for the little courtyard (in this courtyard a broken, dilapidated window frame leaning against the wall, the remains of a box-mattress with the springs hanging out, diverse splinters of wood, the whole observed with a baleful eye) was beyond a doubt less dark. I got up and shook my arms and legs in every direction, or snorted, then set about brushing my clothes off. As I walked around the place, I realized that the light did not come from above, but rather from an oblique slit (either made deliberately or the result of weathering) in the wall, which looked to me to be almost wide enough for a man to slip through. To tell the truth, what attracted my attention to this slit or crack was not so much the brightness I have spoken of as the noise I haven't spoken of, for I could hear an indistinct sound of footfalls and voices, both men's and women's voices, and consequently both men's and women's footfalls. I leaned out, not without difficulty, through the crack to get a look at them (I was practically obliged to lie flat on one forearm, gripping the wall with my other hand). Outside there was countryside, wet and sunny. At least that is what it appeared to me to be, for to tell the truth the thing that especially caught my eye was a plain covered with rounded hillocks and dotted with straggly bushes and heaps of stones. I nonetheless felt like joining them (these men and

45

women) and wandering about this landscape with them, and to encourage myself I called to mind simple and precious joys: walking at a pace that was slow and regular and in perfect rhythm with the trend of the conversation; or that of a thought shared by one of the girls whose presence constituted the charm of this group, nonchalantly pushing a stone with the end of the foot, laughing gaily while looking in each other's faces—and so forth, until tears came to my eyes. The stones were pink and white, and I also wanted to enjoy their warmth. To get through the opening, I had to more or less roll over on my side before getting to the other side, onto the wet and stony ground a bit lower down (its surface was below that of the courtyard, or what I call the courtyard, so that I found that I was, in a manner of speaking, quite high up in relation to my field of vision). This courtyard, in fact, was perhaps some sort of tower, or a blockhouse. The business at hand (getting out of there) was difficult, and I suddenly realized that I was going to have to make several attempts and that my clothes were going to be damaged. Although the members of the group were looking in my direction at this moment, they doubtless had not noticed me before. The girls were dressed in light colors; they were blonde and smiling. They seemed friendly enough to me, but I hesitated to call them over, fearing that I would shock them, for their bright, deep eyes told me that they were used to things that were cheerful and easy. So I drew the half of my body that had already managed to wriggle its way outside back into the blockhouse, somewhat as a snail retreats into its shell. What made me all the more determined was the fact that I recognized one of my former schoolmates among these nonchalant strollers. I couldn't be mistaken. Despite the time that had gone by, the change in the sort of clothes he wore, and the relatively great number of pounds he had put on, it was really he (Coronado), and the permanent menace that had hung over my life as a high-school student, then as a young man, was immediately revived. The class favorite, and doubtless destiny's child as well (and a man of destiny perhaps), strong and clever in battle, with a face that was innocence itself, a face too innocent to let everyone see plainly that he was my tormentor, and that the gentle look in his eye and the appearance of a lover of justice that he assumed in reality concealed endless cruelty. As is probably now understood, this cruelty was taken out on me in particular. Everything he did made me suffer. His continual triumphs (in school, in sports, and morally) in the first place. What I could least forgive him for was his offhand way of going about things, which I did not have. Everything he now has, he took from (me), often by humiliating me. Even when events that allowed him to shine did not concern me, I felt that he was succeeding in all the areas where I myself would have failed. Where I did fail, a fortiori. And when we both succeeded at the same time, his success was perforce more brilliant. And with all my maneuvering, no matter how hard I tried, I was never able to make him take a tumble. Sometimes the rancor that had accumulated within me pushed me to extremes, but these were the times (I would have tried anything) that he disarmed me most easily. It would have been fruitless to try to enlighten others as to his real nature. He would have come out the better for it, and I would have been vanquished, scorned. One day when he was having a fight with the biggest (the strongest) boy in a rival class, even though I was wishing that he (Coronado) would get what was coming to him, I yelled "attaboy, Coronado" along with the others. He fought elegantly and effectively. It was his self-assurance that made him win. I was exasperated. He poisoned my relations at school, for he never stopped disputing my word, showing up my weaknesses, proving me wrong every time he could, that is to say almost every time I opened my mouth. I had never wanted to be either his friend or his enemy, and yet he was present every time that I needed someone to admire me, or at least be willing to overlook my weaknesses. I couldn't challenge him openly, yet one day when I was particularly bitter I tried to provoke him. Following the end of a lively ball game (let's say a soccer game), I attacked one of his teammates, a little Jewish boy who was weaker than I was and whom I despised, out of family tradition on the one hand and cowardice on the other. As I expected, Coronado leaped up. I was counting on having a bitter argument with him that I would win. But instead he punched me in the ear without a word. And now that I was seeing him today with these girls, ten paces away from me, this ear (the right one) again rang or buzzed disagreeably. He had the cruel generosity to let bygones be bygones, ignoring, scorning my repressed hatred, and even going so far as to make me his confidant when he began to hang around with women at the age of fifteen. Not that he flaunted his success. He didn't; but he knew how to raise questions, and each of his exploits seemed natural, each of his successes destined by fate. And there he was square in my path, already there in the midst of other young people that I was trying in vain to get to. The girls were tanned, and had pleasant laughs. I wriggled about, half of my body again poking through the opening. I should perhaps have tried to escape their notice. I couldn't expect any help from anyone. But I might have gotten them to at least leave me in peace. Because of the effort I was making, a stone in the wall knocked loose and rolled down among the other stones. He alone turned around;

he alone spied me. He kicked at the stone and I saw him give a distant, sly, elegant smile. His bright eyes seemed to be drinking the sunlight in.

"Hurry (he shouted) up you blockhead"

There was laughter, even though no one except Coronado had looked my way (and he himself had barely deigned to look at me). And the group went on, leaving me both annoyed and relieved. Soon I could see nothing but the dark line of the first houses in the distance and the rolling countryside. By dint of bruising my ribs, I finally extricated myself from my hiding place, rolling down as the stone had done a few moments before, and finding myself stretched out on my side on the other side of the world. The sky immediately seemed to me to be grayer, and the stones darker, not pink but a dirty, reddish brown. No sun. I got up painfully and felt like going home. This was nothing more nor less than a dingy suburb. It was cold and damp, and became more and more so as I went on. I stuck my hands into the pockets of my raincoat and turned up the collar. There were icy breezes more or less everywhere, and they licked cruelly at my aching arms and legs.

"We (Daniel said) ought to go have a drink somewhere to warm ourselves up

No (I said). I'd better go home

But (he said) if your wife can it'll only take ten minutes it will be better afterward you're silly to think it's so important to quite normal after all for a guy to sometimes go listen we're going to the"

Weak where Cécile was concerned (as I knew I was going to be when I got home), I was equally so where Daniel was concerned, not daring to refuse his invitation for fear I'd look like I didn't have any guts, like I was tied to my wife's apron strings. We sat down on the glassed-in terrace, in a mixture of warm air from the heater and cold air around our feet. On the other side of the square the town hall with its iron gates, its flag, and its clock could be seen. After serving us (a coffee and a glass of draft beer, this latter for me), the waiter had gone back over and stood in front of the door, his hands behind his back, clutching a napkin, nonchalantly whistling a famous accordion tune ("Crystal Pearls" or "Clover" or "Queen of the Dance Hall"). I know of nothing more aggravating than the whistling of an idler when it's cold. Despite the other noises, that's what you hear, for the whistler embroiders on the tune as much as possible in order to get you caught up in it, in this tune and not some other one, so as to drive you out of your mind. I would have liked Daniel to say something, but he said nothing. What could he have said anyway. He was thinking of the same thing I was, seeing the same thing I was. And it was fixed, or engraved, on his mind once and for all. For with this thought and this vision things had stopped for him in his mind, because two series of events had intersected, the course of his life that had brought him to a chair in a café at this precise moment, and the trajectory of this quarry stone that tumbled down from the seventh story of the building, broke through the yellow plastic canopy, and landed on the terrace amid shouts. He had seen his half-empty cup of coffee, with the saucer, the sugar wrapped in paper, and the aluminum spoon came up toward him at top speed and his head instantly cracked open on the table, as on a butcher's block. That is why he couldn't say anything, he whom I had by chance discovered once again in a dingy suburb, after years of silence, on a day when I'd had a bellyful of the lycée. And as in the midst of the horror, among the whistling bullets, with the flash and smoke of shells, and the ground plowed and vomited up by itself, as it were, with the soldiers of the regular army going down the steep slope, brandishing their rifles, their eyes flaming beneath their visors, I tried frantically to lift the headless body of my friend to carry it farther away with me, it was all my past, or what may have been of most value in it, that I was trying to revive, yes, revive, for Daniel had been best man at my wedding, and the only remaining witness of this union (a witness also of my suffering) that Lucile refused. At that point I really lost my way, since despite everything I stubbornly went on dragging this body that made me fall into shell holes time and time again. Perhaps there never were any shells, or any machine guns, but I still have this refusal left, and this terrible smell of warm blood and burned gasoline. This warmth came back to my nostrils once again amid the freezing drafts in this café, in the twilight, opposite the town hall on the other side of the square that can be reached by simply walking across sixty yards of rough gray asphalt, and Daniel, at my side, was neither present nor absent, though he was perhaps really sitting on this chair on the terrace of the café by the town hall sipping expresso that had gotten cold, but then I wasn't there, I was perhaps somewhere else, on some other glassed-in terrace, but all the same the town hall was there opposite me on the other side of the square, with a dark building of dirty brick on the left, with strong iron bars over the windows, and the public park on the right, with iron bars too, and dark trees, and much farther away the dome of its umbrella-shaped kiosk, which had taken on the dusky colors of steel in the rain. It was still drizzling and cold, although spring wasn't far off now, and we immediately had to talk of heating and food. There were four of us, Daniel, another friend, Cécile, and I. We left the town hall and crossed the square, heading for the café. We sat down around an ebonite table. My friends were joking back and forth to make me feel good, but there was no joy in it, and it seemed to me that they exchanged despairing looks from time to time. I repeated their remarks absent-mindedly. And Lucile said nothing. As if nothing had happened. Nothing true, nothing final. So little, that nothing. She withdrew the hand that I had taken in mine. The waiter whistled a famous accordion tune, his hands behind his back, and the leftover beer went flat in our glasses. My ankles were frozen. I looked at the town hall through the glass on which there was reverse writing that I finally deciphered: cold buffet and telephone. The reflection of the lampposts in the puddles of water on the edges of which people were walking heads down, triple men: themselves, their shadows, and their reversed images, or their reflections. Cécile was no longer next to me but across from me, and Coronado was holding her hand, with his other hand on her hip, quite a way down, doubtless caressing the curve of her buttocks, perhaps the two of them had always been like that, a half-smoked cigarette was smoldering in the ash tray. She looked very serious, and puckered her lips and exchanged nice little kisses (oh, kisses) with him, kisses with her puckered lips. They knew that I was there, that I could do nothing to stop them, and that nothing would ever erase this image. I had warned her that I would leave if she cheated on me. She had accepted the bargain, and deliberately chose to see me leave. I shouldn't have come to this café; I wanted to go home. And I had to put up with Coronado's frank smile, a smile embellished by the delicate touch of Cécile's kiss, and Cécile's scornful look before she left, and the words that I wanted to say, to the effect that I had perhaps merely imagined that the wedding ceremony had taken place, stuck in my throat, in a painful knotted ball. I also had to beg the pardon of the waiter barring the doorway, and he gave a disagreeable growl before ungraciously moving aside. I cut across the square, avoiding looking at the town hall, and entered the public park. From the inside it looks immense, much larger than it did from the outside. Winding paths ran across a sorry-looking lawn dotted with scraggly bushes, the whole crowned by irregularly planted trees with trunks circled with iron. Night was slow in coming, as if the day were trying to last longer than it should have, although it was perhaps still the month of February. As I went on, the benches and the flower beds disappeared, the paths became indistinct, and patches of grass overran the gravel. This neglected (or even abandoned) end of the park overlooked, in fact, an expanse of empty lots that could be seen (or made out) indistinctly between the trees. Then from far off but still discernible, there came to my ears the whining and somewhat broken music of some sort of mechanical instrument (not necessarily a hand organ). The counterpoint of the bass notes first, then little by little all the lines of the harmony. The rhythm: triple time. The melody: cyclical. I went toward the singsong sound, and soon found myself standing exactly on the borderline between the park and the vacant lots. On the left, parked next to the iron fence, was a large light truck, covered with dark-green paint that was rough and peeling off in spots. On the side of the truck was a sign in white paint that read: ATTRACTIONS KAMIEN. On the right was the merry-go-round. Except for the figures (or subjects) on it and the raised canvas, everything that could be painted—roof, floor, iron mountings—had been painted with the same rough dark-green paint. The merry-go-round was in operation, though there was no one on it. Kamien (it could only be he) was sitting in the middle of it, in thick gray flannel pants and with his chest protected, despite the cold, only by a navy blue vest, from which hung two muscular, knotted arms. And his empty gaze was not focused on anything, neither on me nor the truck nor the merry-go-round, no, not on anything. In the man's hard, fixed stare, still focused somewhere else, I nonetheless recognized the soul of a soldier. Yes, this man seemed to me to be a hero. He was fighting the same battle that I was, with neither hope nor despair. But despite their number and their strategic power (thanks to the tanks, the airplanes, the flame throwers, and the modern machine guns lent by Hitler so that they could be tested) the Fascists would have to retreat before us (or remain pinned down) for at least a second, I mean perhaps for only a second. And during this extraordinary second we shall stand our ground, and even advance, thanks to the materiel going past up ahead, and not just on parade—bicycles, horses, two little cars, a tank, yes, a tank, with a little revolving turret on top that is also a machine gun, and even an old fire truck that may still be of some use. This iron barrier will be thrown up right in your fac.., and your hesitation will be our sole and final victory. And all during this time, as this old dream comes back to us, Kamien is quietly puffing on his pipe, unconcerned about the cold and the danger, as if nothing were going to happen, Kamien, Kamien, Kamien. I sat down on the only bench nearby, the one where mothers wait for their children, but there is no mother waiting tonight, the soldiers aren't back from the war (they won't be back) and their women have other children by other men. No mother waits for her kid as she watches him gallop on a wooden horse, because it's wartime, and the children are hidden in caves tonight, and for several days to come, and perhaps, if everything goes well, for several months, and because the republicans need all those things, and because these horses of another age, these rattling bicycles, all this rusty steel that creaks at every turn, are not for kids anyway, all of it, in fact, having been requisitioned, although there are no uniforms, although nobody speaks the same language (they came from all over, and often with no faith in the cause, because they had nothing better to do, or simply because they were cucko..). Kamien . . . let the procession go by, once, twice, three times. It'll come by many times more. Alongside his left foot, squares of perforated cardboard (that's what makes the music), bound together with paper tape, are heaped one on top of the other, evenly, like neatly piled calling cards. Over on the other side of the iron fence, an elegant woman goes by, her neck hunched down in a charming fur collar because she's chilly. My eyes follow her until she disappears at a brisk pace, her breasts trembling slightly with each stride, and as I watch her I think of the warm intimacy of a bed on this winter evening. But I don't exist for her, not now anyway, for she disappears behind the truck without turning her eyes. A few more times around, Kamien, and you'll have to stop, for nobody else will come along today, and the two of us are all alone, you the Pole, me the Frenchman, the two of us will have to stand our ground all by ourselves, and advance if possible. Toward the south, yes, we'll go south, dragging these broken-down machines to the very end. He doesn't turn on the lights because there are no lights. He suddenly gets up, and the circling and the music stop. He now crosses the path, rummages in the truck, and comes back with various tools. I have gotten up too. He holds out a big pair of pliers and a little sack. The pliers are to unscrew the bolts and the canvas so as not to lose them. We dismantle the merry-go-round piece by piece, the so-called Attractions Kamien (the "s" of the plural is a come-on; the one and only thing Kamien pos-

55

sesses, probably, is this merry-go-round, and it may be that he stole it, and the truck too, this being the reason why he covered everything over with a rough coat of dark-green paint that's peeling because he didn't have the patience to scrape and sand the old paint off). One by one, we carry all the pieces of the mechanism to the truck, or rather I carry them and he puts them away, for he's the only one who knows where things belong. We're done. All that remains is a lighter spot (a round one, because the mixture of dust and gravel here didn't get wet in the rain) in the place where Kamien's carnival was being held an hour ago, a spot that's hardly visible now, because the rain, a light icy rain, is beginning to fall again and it's getting darker. The tailgate rattles as it closes. Kamien bounds into the driver's cab, slips a heavy leather jacket over his leather vest, holding the strap of a haversack between his teeth. We sit down on the ground behind the truck, somewhat protected from the wind and the rain by the overhang of the truck. He offers me a snack which I refuse. I refuse brandy too. He eats quietly, with a hearty appetite (without hurrying), bringing the neck of the bottle of brandy to his lips frequently. At last he gives one deliberate, powerful belch, a sort of very scornful profession of faith, and goes about the business of lighting his pipe, an operation which I follow with interest, counting the matches, eleven in all, while I smoke my Gauloises. We say nothing. I soon understood that Kamien would never be able to talk to me. He is a Pole, as I have said, and doesn't know a word of French. Besides, what's the point of it (it is quite true that the republicans couldn't understand each other). Kamien finally gets up, brushes off the crumbs all over his pants, and with one last belch picks up his bottle and his haversack, closes the front of his jacket over his neck, and enters the cab again.

The door squeaks as it closes behind him. I climb up in turn into the back of the truck and bed myself down, stretching out as far as I can among the horses and the bicycles, with my head resting on a piece of rolled-up canvas. Goodnight. Goodnight, Lucile. Oh my Go . . , the warm intimacy of the bed, Cécile, with one of my hands pressing your left breast, the other your ass, and the slow sliding of one flesh against another (mine and yours, I mean), and then at the end that heavy and peaceful sleep, but good heavens, just look how I. The seat of the cab creaks, Kamien coughs and farts, and I raise my head halfway up. The soldier's lot for me. Since I'm going off to war, it is quite natural for my wife to, yes, it's quite natural. All the same, Cécile, the little whor. . . All the same, Cécile.

At dawn next morning the hiccuping rumble of the motor replaced Kamien's snoring after an intermezzo of assorted belches, farts, and various other eructations. I climbed into the cab, which was all warm and stinking, and sat down in the passenger's seat. We crossed a series of empty lots, and the back of Kamien's head vibrated in rhythm to the bumps we went over with a great noise of sick sheet metal. Then we came to an endless (and even unended) gray suburb, and Kamien took advantage of this opportunity to stop and get gas. At the same time he also regulated his blood pressure by absorbing several swallows of brandy. All I did was have a smoke. We rolled on all day, stopping only once to have a lunch and take a leak (I lunched and did not neglect to take a leak) at a truck stop. We slept that night as we had the night before, but I was so dead on my feet that this time I agreed to share Kamien's snack, which did not seem to please him particularly, and even to drink a little brandy, a stock of which, I noticed, he kept under the front seat. We had camped a little way from a bleak village on a plain (a bleak plain too), in a spot that had a sign reading: camping permitted (peeling black paint on worm-eaten wood). The next day we set up the merry-go-round in the square as several kids in smocks looked on, their faces blue with the cold. The merry-go-round went round and round all afternoon, but to tell the truth we had few customers. Mothers would approach us cautiously (scowling at us), slowly read the dirty placard announcing how much each ride cost, with a re-duced price for three rides, sometimes standing there for quite a while, and usually going away dragging their brats behind them, or else counting and recounting a few coins that they took out of their smocks. Kamien collected the money. I operated the machinery, and Ka-mien came to join me in the middle to run the music. He had put his leather vest on again, and the women (certain ones) watched his muscles ripple beneath his reddened skin. There was a ritual: the kids pulled the tails off the horses (which seemed to be removable, for after each ride Kamien brought these animals their hairy appendages back as he collected the money), and used them as whips to slash Kamien in the face, and he responded, without so much as a smile, by smacking their bottoms with a little broom. The day passed very quickly. That evening he appeared to be totting up the figures, and he gave me my share: five hundred francs for the day (five new francs, or five francs). Then he dis-apeared inside Le Grand Hôtel du Lion d'Or facing the town hall, after putting on his jacket. The next day when I climbed up into the cab, he was still asleep, surrounded by the smell of stale brandy. He painfully slid across into the passenger's seat (as I went through contortions to let him slide past), half opening his eyes and rapping several times on the wheel with the heel of his hand, meaning by this simple language that he would leave the driving up to me. So I got into the driver's seat and started the motor. I drove south.

This is what our days were like, and little by little, if the daily take permitted it, he raised both my wages and the number of duties I was to perform, so that at the very end all he had left was the title of captain, being satisfied merely to take care of the money, while I drove the truck, took care of putting the machinery up and taking it down, and running the merry-go-round and even the music. Even so, when it was time for work (for me to, I mean) he still took off his leather jacket so as to show off a navy blue leather vest, but after that he was content to watch me as he drew on his pipe and sipped his brandy while I brought him the money we'd taken in, which he immediately pocketed. Though it was almost April, it still froze every night. There were more rolling hills now, and there were already signs of the stony soil of the south of France. Muffled rumblings from the south sometimes reached our ears when the wind carried them to us, and each day they became more distinct. I sometimes said to myself that we'd have to fight, but the first battle was waged long before I thought it would be. It happened very late one evening in the vast back room of a poorly lighted café. I was writing a letter to Cécile, on a table of dark-red ebonite, sitting on a bench upholstered in an expensive imitation leather (but it wasn't leather) fabric that I believe is called moleskin, drinking a glass of beer, or rather I was trying for the hundredth time to write this letter, and had therefore written "My dear Cécile" on the top of a blank page (in those days I used an enormous quantity of paper, for the reason that I have just indicated, and I wanted it to be handsome, very handsome paper) for the hundredth time. From time to time the exclamations of the billiard players rang out from the center of this room full of nothing but men, and I then craned my neck to watch the game. Kamien was somewhere in the room drinking coffee, or to put it more exactly, endlessly pouring brandy from his own bottle into his coffee.

(A man had planted himself there four paces away from me turning his back to me with his legs apart his two arms dangling and two others were a little behind him on his right one of them halfway perched on the billiard table where no one was playing now the other whom I saw in profile was biting his nails come on let me fix you up you fuckin' Polack you dirty Polack bastard Kamien sat there not moving for a moment then I saw him get up and puff nervously at his pipe that had gone out he took two steps forward and stuck his hand into his pocket it wasn't a box of matches that he pulled out a big box of safety matches but a shiny knife with a cruel glint which was a miracle moreover for never that I know of had Kamien ever possessed anything clean nothing but worn and dirty objects that was as far as he got for the fingernail biter had seen his chance and moved behind him and was holding him around the waist while the billiard man disarmed him relieved him of his fine knife they had a firm hold on him and were restraining him without any apparent difficulty what's more for Kamien now remained perfectly still like certain steers at the slaughterhouse not all but some Kamien resembled the former even though the third one the cowboy that's what I call him because of his rather theatrical I mean cinematic pose that I described a moment ago was hammering at his face his ribs his belly his feet with a methodical rain of blows punctuated by shouts at the top of his lungs and the noise of blows on bruised flesh had a disagreeable effect on me he had fainted a moment before they let him slip to the floor Kamien looked at me just once with the gaze of a sick

60

animal I was sure I was the one he was looking at but I didn't budge one of them picked up the knife and stuck it in his pocket.)

The nail biter came up to my table, and cleared off the table top with a sweeping gesture knocking off my glass of beer which broke on the floor with a delicate, silvery sound. On the spattered sheet of my stationery tablet I then wrote, keeping myself from trembling: "My dear Lucile, Kamien died like a hero." They left the bistro with a mechanical stride, and a brazen look all around. It grew noisy again and conversations started up. The big balls (two white and one red) clicked against each other. Only then did I fold my letter four times, put it carefully in the pocket of my suit coat, get up from the table, and go lean over Kamien. I grabbed him by the armpits, pulled him over to the wall as best I could, and leaned him up against it. He opened a bleary eye and held out his hand, and I went over and got his bottle, which was still three-quarters full. I put the neck of it in his mouth, tipping it at the right angle, and he grabbed it with an unsteady hand. I sat down on the floor next to him, and we waited for dawn. Little by little the room emptied, and soon we were alone. I had to go out once into the icy night to get another bottle out from under the front seat of our truck. I helped him drink until four A.M. He accepted my help docilely, mechanically. I then tried to help him get up so that we could go back to our home away from home. But he sat there stubbornly, bent over double. By working terribly hard at it, I managed to get him on his feet, but he immediately began to vomit, a really fantastic amount, everything: what he had drunk, what he had eaten for dinner in this café, and at the end a bit of blood, a sort of pinkish foam that he brought up in little spasms. I was obliged to let go of him; he slid down gently, still hiccuping a bit, but the spasms finally stopped. He fell to the ground once and for all. Dead drunk, or rather drunk and dead. I went to the door, stepping over the pools of vomit, got in the cab which now was mine, and slept like a log, first locking the doors. Violent taps on the windows woke me with a start. I raised my head and saw the face of a man all upset about something standing out against the pale light of dawn and making broad gestures with his hand every time he stopped hammering on the door or frantically rattling the door handle. I finally opened the door, although I really didn't want to, allowing him time to jump off the running board to get out of the way. He slowly climbed back up, and brought his face close to mine.

"Are you (he said) the Polack's pal"

I didn't answer, never having had, so far as I know, any sort of friendly relations with Kamien, never once having exchanged a word with him, and for a good reason, so that it sometimes seemed to me, as it did this morning for example, that I had completely lost the power of speech.

"All right (he said) you're his associate the Polack is dead you'll have the cops on your tai.. it's not a very pleasant sight what did they do to him I saw him you'd better leave right away instead of sitting there like an idiot"

I made a vague gesture with my hand (vague to me, especially, for I didn't mean anything by this gesture) and he must have thought it meant that I didn't know where to go. He was kind enough to offer me his help.

"You (he said) have only to come in with us come with the troupe etc."

That I didn't look particularly bright, but that they'd find something I could do, that I would eat with the others, that they worked as a team and for everybody's

common benefit, that the manager of the troupe (Chataignon) would take care of the transportation and the
maintenance of the merry-go-round, the profits of which
would be shared by everybody, that if that didn't suit
me it didn't much matter because I was going to have
the cops after me, whereas with them I would be guar-
anteed a job and wouldn't risk being picked up for
vagrancy. I was sleepy.

"It (he said) would be better to leave right away so
as to catch up with the others."

And he pushed me over so as to get behind the wheel
himself. I wanted nothing but to be allowed to sleep.
And as a matter of fact, I managed to sleep all day, and
also that night. Little by little I met the various members of the troupe, a small troupe, I must say, in the
face of a powerful, well-armed enemy. (Monsieur)
Chataignon, the manager, and his wife, the man with the
beret (the one who had come to get me) and his wife,
(Monsieur) Alexis, the Negro, and another woman who
did gymnastics on the rings and the horizontal bar, and
danced besides, but I couldn't tell you what kind of
dancing. We put on the whole show ourselves: a shooting gallery (clay pipes, paper flowers, bottles of spar-
kling wine), a tent with tiers of seats, with a flamboyant
pennant (The Giants of the Ring) flying above the platform where the pitch was made, and finally my merry-
go-round. The whole thing bumped and pitched its way
south in search of good weather. The first time that
someone tried to start up Kamien's music, the mechanism broke for good with one last sob, and the painted
wooden box was relegated to the back of the truck
(which had been repainted immediately: Attractions
Chataignon, and the license plates changed), and never
came out again. I soon realized why they had welcomed
me so cordially. A member of the troupe had dropped

out. As a matter of fact, Alexis's missing partner was none other than Kamien's principal adversary, and he had disappeared after the fight without even asking for his pay. The trapeze artist was nice enough to explain all this to me one night in the cab of the truck, which I was still using as a place to sleep. She also told me that I should take over the role of Alexis's partner, for if I didn't they would no longer be able to put up the tent because Alexis's solo turn wasn't a big enough attraction to draw customers, and said that I was handsome enough and strong enough to give people a thrill as I faced Monsieur Alexis, that there was no trick to it, that I always looked sad and that I ought to mix with the others more, that everybody was counting on me, that if something was bothering me I had only to confide in her, that she came from the south and not from the north as people might guess from her hair, that her name was.

"I (I said) believe I've already met you your name is Cécilia
My name (she said) is Julienne Lucie (Lucile) Augustine Claudette Clara and my name is also Cécilia take your hand away you're very nice not now it's the wrong time of the month it wouldn't be clean you're going to get me dirty you're going to try out tomorrow with Alexis he'll explain everything he's not a bad sort at all no I said it's the wrong time of the month everybody is counting on you you're making me cold you have cold hands come on good night."

The next day I took on the functions of a sparring partner for two thousand francs (20 NF, or twenty Francs) a day, plus a seventh of the money taken in by the merry-go-round, which I no longer ran. The wife of the man with the beret (who ran the shooting gallery), the oldest of the women, took it over from me, though she didn't use the little broom, so that little by little the brown jute tails of the horses disappeared. (Monsieur) Chataignon was both the manager and the master of ceremonies: he occupied the center of the platform, brandishing a tinny-sounding microphone that he literally shouted into, half strangling himself and sputtering vigorously between one dance-hall tune and the next, with Cécilia, who danced for the pitch, on his right in a tutu, and on his left (Monsieur) Alexis in a Negro boxer's outfit (red metallic trunks, high yellow shoes) jumping about and smacking his gloves together, looking terribly thin and almost frozen to death, while Madame Chataignon took care of collecting the money. As for me, I mingled with the crowd and waited for the moment to make my appearance.

"Step right up (Chataignon would shout) you young people come on in and see the favorite show of young sports fans of real young people (etc.) first of all Madame Cécilia (this was the name she now went by) who is out here dancing for your pleasure but inside she will perform the most perilous the most amazing feats for at the risk of her life Cécilia is able to do gymnastic feats that no professional athlete not even men athletes ever attempt moreover young people simply because we like this city because we like the folks who live around here we have decided that for just this one time we will make a sacrifice yes a great sacrifice that we do not hesitate to make for you as an extra added attraction you will be permitted today to see the greatest boxer of all time or at least one of the greatest several times a champion and never beaten that is to say he's never lost a single bout a man whose technique and courage have no equal who retired from a professional career only because he despised the fakery and the trickery that unfortunately occur too often in professional boxing I mean Monsieur

Alexis who is up here with us come on Champ come and say hello to your public you may applaud young people he deserves it the champ is here tonight only for the sake of this fine sport but it will not be just an exhibition it will be a real fight but that's not all if among you young people there are courageous and willing men whatever your age and weight you have the unusual opportunity tonight of facing Monsieur Alexis the champ right here in person that is to say Monsieur Alexis agrees to meet you in three rounds of three minutes each but that's not all this evening simply because we are in this city the management agrees to award a prize of five thousand francs * that's right five thousand francs to the winner of this fight and perhaps this winner will be the brave man who will succeed in getting to Monsieur Alexis let's get on with the show folks the fight will be conducted according to the sporting traditions of boxing which have caused real boxing to be sometimes known as the noble art step right up folks step right up I'm going to ask Monsieur Alexis to give me a pair of boxing gloves there we are I'll unfasten one of them and throw it to the man worthy of the name who will please pick it up"

That was my cue to come into the picture (me). I raise my hand and shout to Chataignon who waves the glove above his head. People for the most part immediately look at me with surprise, mistrust, or respect, and stand away from me and fall silent. Chataignon, up on the platform, pretends to be just as surprised, while Alexis appears to be looking me over like a connoisseur. Then:

"Monsieur (Chataignon says) takes up the gauntlet

---

* NF 50, fifty Francs.

give courage like that a big hand folks that's a real man monsieur I throw you the glove"

I try as hard as I can to catch it handily, but usually pick it up off the ground, unless some obliging soul passes it to me, and then I make my way toward the platform. Alexis nobly holds out his hand to help me up onto the platform (and then the folks sometimes do give me a big hand) and I place myself on Chataignon's right. He says:

"Monsieur, will you tell us your age and weight?"

I say: "Twenty-seven years old, sixty-seven kilos."

(I wanted to say "kilograms" but Chataignon declined this suggestion, claiming that it would sound pedantic.)

He says: "You've never boxed professionally?"

I say: "No."

He says: "Do you swear on your word of honor?"

I say: "Yes."

He says: "So tonight you are going to face Monsieur Alexis for three three-minute rounds before the eyes of this fine audience, these fine folks."

I say: " . . . "

He says: "Do you promise to fight a good clean fight?"

I say: "Yes, I want to knock that dirty nigger's block off."

He says: "Ah monsieur, ah monsieur, monsieur, that's not nice, that's not nice at all, you should be ashamed to talk like that at your age, yes indeed, I don't know where you were brought up, but I shall take the liberty of saying that you are what is vulgarly known as a dirty bastar.., yes, that's right, a dirty bastar.., and at that I'm being too easy on you."

The crowd gets a little worked up, and Cécilia calls me names in a loud voice. Alexis steps over toward me with a threatening look, and Chataignon has to step between us so that the fight won't start on the spot (in which case he'd lose his take).

He goes on: "You'll settle it inside in the ring, that's where you'll see real men, that's where we'll be waiting for you, and rest assured, Monsieur Alexis will see to it that you get what's coming to you, he'll teach you a real lesson, you won't come back for more, and what's more it seems to me that I've seen you before, you may well be one of those professionals who follow carnivals around to pick up prizes, but this time you're going to have a real fight on your hands, go get ready, gentlemen, while the sports fans of this fine place take their seats after having paid the modest entry fee of one Franc,* it's a spectacle well worth seeing, an unusual and sporting fight, step right up, come see the favorite attraction of young people with sporting blood, this is real sport."

And while the dance-hall music plays and Chataignon wipes his mouth on the back of his sleeve, I go get ready in the wings, that is to say I bare my torso, but naturally keep my pants on, and put on a pair of leather gloves that appear to have undergone repeated assaults by an enraged cat, they're so full of scratches, and terribly heavy. First comes Cécilia's perilous number on a cross-beam above the ring: a full turn on the rings, the grand circle and recovery on the horizontal bar, and the same on the trapeze (corresponding music: a Spanish *paso doble*). Chataignon takes off his splendid jacket (Jazz: "Tiger Rag"), loosens his tie, and climbs over the ropes up into the ring to act as referee. He stretches out his arms to quiet the crowd, and if he's in good form he starts spieling again, while I shout in my corner and Alexis jumps up and down in his to relax his muscles. A bell rings, and there is silence. I walk toward my adver-

---

* One hundred old francs (or 1 NF).

sary, looking as mean as I can, awkwardly guarding myself, and Alexis's number consists of ridiculing me with a relentless and professional display of his technique, which hardly hurts me at all. He circles around me, jumping all the while, his head swinging constantly from right to left (and from left to right) and his arms waving like the legs of a mad insect. He nimbly parries the blows I try to land on him, for the greater joy of the audience, and finally he hits me in the face just before the bell announcing the end of the round. I don't like this part at all. Stools are passed in to us, we each sit in our corners, Alexis gives the audience a smile that shows all his fine white teeth, and coughs into his glove. The bell rings, I get up (looking furious). Alexis is less nimble, my hectic blows seem to find their mark, the audience gets all excited, I corner him against the ropes, ostensibly get my energy back, and hit him below the belt (on his hip, really). Alexis raises his arms, then bends over double, with his face frozen in a hideous grin of pain. I raise my arms in turn and hail the spectators who boo (a low blow, but perhaps it pleases the racists) and Chataignon counts to seven. Alexis is hard put to it to get up and face me, but I pitilessly pursue my advantage. The bell fortunately ends his troubles. The third act is the one where punishment gets dished out (my punishment). Alexis deliberately walks all over me and employs all the resources of his art, sometimes even taking his role of a lover of justice seriously. I flee, he runs after me, and presses me so hard that I finally fall to the canvas, beaten (and it serves me right), while Chataignon counts to ten, runs over to Alexis, raises his arm, and proclaims him the winner. Then Alexis holds out his hand to me, helps me get up, and generously embraces me, coughing the while. The show is over, I'm freezing cold, I go get dressed. One evening Alexis punished me harder than usual and just to get his goat I let myself fall down again instead of standing up to receive his embrace. Chataignon hurriedly chased everyone out, but I was already putting my clothes back on when he came over to me, not at all happy.

"I (I said) don't like nosebleeds Monsieur Alexis will have to understand that that is very unpleasant for me if not I'll defend myself the next time and I won't guarantee anything in that case I'm in too much pain to have dinner with you tonight I'm going to go rest if I'm mistreated like this my state of health may not permit me to keep this job very long I advise you to think it over"

And I tottered off to my cab, which I was still using as a place to sleep. Cécilia soon came to join me with a little basin of warm water and a basket of food. She gently bathed my face, and the two of us devoured the food in the basket. I told her how I hated violence, how I loved the Republic, which had to be saved, the goo.. lor.. only knows. She caressed my hand as she listened, and I asked her if it was the wrong time of the month, no of course not, if she would like to, yes of course, and I spread her coat out on the seat and knelt down on the floor, with the steering wheel in my back, and took off her skirt and sweater; I found her breasts small and warm, the hairs of her pubis made my rod tingle, and we made love as long as I was able to, until I gave in and went to sleep, drunk with fatigue, my fly wet, my limbs exhausted and the skin broken from knocking against her as I worked her over.

We had been sleeping for about two hours (or perhaps even three or four) when a slight noise woke me up. I wiped the moisture off the windshield and saw a thin black shadow circling the truck in the fog. Cécilia woke up too just about then and opened the door.

"What (she said in an irritated voice) are you doing there you're going to get cold

You (he said) are my wife I want you back

Go (she said) away

You (he said) 're coming to sleep with me period

Let (she said) me alone

You (he said) shouldn't be here with him

What (she said) I do is none of your business

That's (I said) right we're telling you it's none of your business

Claoua (he said) is my wife not yours she's got to come with me period"

But Cécilia closed the door again and stretched out on top of me, caressing my cock until it was hard enough to get in her, and outside there were no more footfalls, but now and again as the springs of the seat gave a louder squeak we heard the other guy whine: Claoua, you're my wife I want you back.* In the morning we found him asleep on the running board.† That night he refused to do his number at first, saying that he was cold, that he was tired, and Chataignon, after having bawled him out, gave him permission to go on in his dressing gown (an old bathrobe really), with the one complaint that this hid a large part of the champ's anatomy (what you've got to show them, the women especially, is muscles).

"Fuc.. (Alexis replied with an expressive gesture) having my muscles show I don't feel like kicking the bucket just for you"

He didn't feel like it, yet every time he coughed, with a sad, sick look in his eyes, he was closer to kicking off.

---

* Period.
† *Idem.*

Neither of us followed the usual scenario that Chataignon had thought up and staged. He had no idea what was going on and called us names under his breath. Finally he hurriedly declared Alexis the winner on points, though I had just hit him square in the chest as hard as I could, pushing me away so that I wouldn't do it again and muttering that I was a dirty bastar . . , raising Alexis's hand as Alexis kept hiccuping, and calling him a miserable cucko . . and a god-damned nigger as the audience hooted (fake, etc.). We finally all gathered in the manager's trailer. I arrived last, not at all displeased with myself. They were all leaning over in a circle around Alexis, who was stretched out on a bench moaning and coughing and spitting blood into an old handkerchief he was pressing against his mouth.

"Go (the manager said) get a grog and two aspirins from the café

Pardon (I said) me sir but aspirin won't be enough in this case it would be better to call a doctor for this man is seriously ill perhaps even very seriously ill he probably has tuberculosis

Shut (Alexis said, raising his head) your trap fuc . . you I don't have tuberculosis period

You (Chataignon said) heard what he said he doesn't have tuberculosis so shut up it's only a touch of the flu

It's (Alexis said) a touch of the flu period"

I went off. Cécilia had it in for me and didn't come to see me, in spite of what she'd promised the night before. Chataignon sent the man in the beret over to tell me that I was a dirty bastard, that if I kept hitting Alexis and making an ass of myself he'd take care of me personally and would even go so far as to fire me from the troupe, and that he wasn't about to tell me so again. Then everything blew over. The whole thing was forgotten. Cécilia came to see me again, but I finally realized

that I wasn't the only one enjoying her favors, for one night when Madame Chataignon had gone to visit a relative in a town we were passing through, I found Alexis rolled up in a ball under the manager's trailer whining: "I want you back, you're my wife, period." I then sat down on the running board and the two of us began to sing the following two verses in plainsong:
He:

Claoua/ come sleep with me/ you're my wife/ period

Me:

Cécilia/ come sleep with me/ you're my wife/ period

et cetera . . .

We were still traveling south. The days grew longer, the air was getting imperceptibly warmer. As the sky took on red and blue shadings and we neared the horizon, the rumblings (from the battlefield) became more distinct, and we could hear them quite plainly when the sound of the motors or the yells of the crowd died down. And the fact that we were in danger, or rather being rejected, grew more obvious every day. The audiences grew nastier and nastier, a sign that we were already in hostile country. Yet we went on. We went on until we were put to flight, which I think happened one night in June. The twilight was magnificent, I wish I could describe it, as shimmering and vibrant as the base string of a guitar when one quietly plucks it with the ball of the thumb, and the ramparts of the ancient city with their ocher stone seemed to have been built for this evening, for living this day but not beyond it: I don't remember the date exactly, but I know that it felt like vacation time. The girl, the little girl that I had dragged by the hand through all this beauty, the sea, the sand, the rocks, into villages with Romanesque tiles, between white walls, on burning, golden paths, whom today I was still pursuing in the same décor, after her betrayal, and who kept fleeing endlessly, forgetting me endlessly, forgetful of my caresses and of her caresses and therefore of ourselves, tourists in rags and tatters, dusty and healthy, tanned and sturdy, as we mingled with this warm atmosphere that suited this country perfectly, in short, almost naked, lover and beloved, considered handsome, adopted, perennial vacationers, unusual vacationers—who had disappeared, I, yesterday a young teacher with a fine future before him, today a sharpshooter and a fake harlequin with dirty sweating feet, Cécile, my Spain, there a hundred paces away, facing the ramparts tinged with yellow, red, and blue, her tan face lifted toward a silhouette patrolling the road, but it wasn't me, it could have been but it wasn't, it no longer was, so I shouted: "Lucile," and she turned around slowly, and someone (Madame Chataignon) pulled me by the arm and told me that it was time for my act, that she had been looking everywhere for me and that her husband was obliged to make the pitch last longer, but that people were about to leave, and Cécile sat down on the sidewalk, and I realized that she was suffering, and I tried to get closer to her, but the other person drew me back, and Cécile must have seen, and I was suffering too, and the silhouette was now climbing down the ramparts on a stone ladder, holding out his hands, and Cécile had a white stone in the form of a heart in her hands and was frantically striking it against the worn stone of the sidewalk, her eyes avoiding mine, and then I turned away and passed my hand in front of my eyes to erase the chimerical vision of a deceitful little girl with dirty hands and knees, sitting on the ground, who was suffering because I was leaving, knowing why I was leaving, and not knowing, not wanting to know, Cécile, my wife who was almost a child. But my pain

74

was all the more terrible in that she was rediscovered (in that I rediscovered her) such as she had been, while I had become what I was, once and for all, having been dragged away by Madame Chataignon. The carnival hands had set themselves up outside the ramparts, near the canal, and not inside the city, by order of the mayor. We had joined other troupes: there were all sorts of things, all sorts of merry-go-rounds, in fact every sort of carnival attraction, and a fireworks show had even been prepared. I went over toward our tent, The Giants of the Ring, and mingled with a crowd that was already fairly excited, waiting for the glove. When I raised my hand, though, there were about twenty other eager and determined candidates, but Chataignon naturally singled me out despite them. He threw the glove toward me, but everyone crowded in to catch it.

"Will (Chataignon shouted into his microphone) you please let monsieur have it please
Give (I shouted) it to me"

I finally got it, though I risked being trampled to death. Then an uproar began that sounded like heckling. For from that moment on everything happened as if by plan. The pitch was shortened. Chataignon's voice (Please calm down, folks, I beg you) was lost amid the shouts of the audience, he seemed to founder in the sea of people, and the dance-hall music started up. Most of the people passed through the turnstile without paying. I made my way inside as best I could, clutching my precious glove under my arm, and climbed into the ring. Alexis was already there, amid catcalls and whistles. We didn't even exchange ten blows. Alexis was coughing even more than usual. Then suddenly there was a short silence, then a terrifying rumble or roar that made the tiers of seats tremble, a detachment of heavy tanks seemed to be descending on us, and there were shouts of "send 'em to the toilets" to the rhythm of feet stamping the floor. Alexis staggered and coughed again, holding his chest. Then all of a sudden a riot broke out. Everybody got up, stampeded toward the ring, and tried to box with the champion. Monsieur Alexis, his arms dangling, his gaping mouth showing his teeth, remained on his feet for ten seconds, bleeding, his eyes vacant, before being stomped underfoot. Then the troupe rushed in, weapons in hand. I heard the first shots and saw people who had climbed up on the tent poles let go and fall onto the seats and into the ring. Then, I assure you, there was a rain of thousands of knives, driven by the wind from the machine guns. And the tent fell on top of the whole thing. I had grabbed a wooden club and was laying to in front of me and around me to make a path for myself. In spite of a violent blow in the back I managed to wriggle out, flat on my stomach, and saw the battle. The horizon cracked, red, green, orange, and blue stars rained down on us, you could hear the cannon and the machine guns, and the flashes from them showed us death watching us from the top of the cracked towers, and the troupe was now advancing, their bayonets at the ready and the stocks of their rifles firmly anchored between hip and elbow. And the plain groaned beneath their feet, and the streets disintegrated, and the strings of the guitars broke. I saw them advancing, their heads raised high, concealing beneath their masks an obscure geometry of smothered firebrands. And then the shouts, and this odor of powder and blood, and this woman felled with a saber blow, whose groans I heard distinctly despite the uproar. They came in methodical waves, and their eyes gleamed with the same steely brilliance as their arms, pitiless and beautiful, implored or applauded, dizzying conquerors, bloody comets. An explosion of noise and light revealed Cécilia to me, I ran toward her, grabbed her by the arm, and we galloped to the truck. I started the engine and pushed forward, trying to forget the crackling noise of dead or dying bodies beneath the wheels. We drove along a canal, but the uproar followed us for a long time before dying away: the cries of distress and triumph, the music, the shots, the deep, heavy detonations of the cannon firing round after round. But when we turned around, above the city dying beneath its stone we could still see the sky light up spasmodically, as if there were heat lightning. We drove far into the night, finally stopping in an inn where they were willing to rent us a room. But Cécilia said no not tonight, leave me alone, I said let me alone, I'm tired, and finally she went to sleep. I had a stomachache all night long, and got up a hundred times, my belly rent and in a cold sweat. When I too finally fell asleep a square of daylight was showing through the curtains. And when I awoke, Cécile had disappeared. I got up and dressed hurriedly, then went down into the dining room.

"Do you (I asked) know

No (he replied) she didn't say a word she ate a leisurely breakfast she had a date with a guide yes a young man yes she seemed to know him slightly sort of Spanish looking yes kind and generous yes I think so that was at least three hours ago"

Three hours too late as usual, the day I got home and found Coronado there, three hours too late afterward too, too late to run.

(That's right you can pay the bill eat a leisurely breakfast as she did dry buttered toast cardboard croissants one third coffee two thirds milk and two lumps of sugar a cigarette then Lucile's suitcase isn't in the trunk of the car any more I should have suspected that guide is a

77

trick she's gone across the border and not just for a simple outing even the good luck charm she hung on the rearview mirror is gone
You haven't by any chance seen a lady who
How do you expect me to
There are so many of them no I
Have you
No no one
Have you by any chance
Hundreds
A couple only a few couples
We're not here to
Fill 'er up
The windshield too
Have you by any chance
So many people cross the border
Pardon me officer have you
First of all what have you to declare let me see that
If it were only raining I could stop at all the inns she doesn't like to travel when the weather's bad she's afraid the car will be hit by lightning but whom can I ask they talk too much and don't say anything and the others soldiers too many of them with a cold and hostile look in their eye dressed in green khaki and black leather armed to the teeth hiding in the dusty bushes burning in the sun I have a headache)

On the hills bordering the road a flock of black sheep was watching the city. I had a headache.

(Pasajes de San Juan puerto a dark narrow alley unevenly paved between high houses with multicolored clothes hung out to dry the passers-by hug the walls as I drive by on my way to the harbor I have a headache and each paving stone sets a little luminous hammer going under the top of my skull the street rises sharply you can already see the wharf and above it the masts of

the boats gently swaying what is that idiot with a basket
on a bicycle doing he'll have to stop I'm taking up all the
room but he's coming down toward me faster and faster
I press the brake pedal down hard and let up on the
throttle he lets go of his basket raises his two arms hits
the hood and makes a resounding noise the bicycle
turned over as he landed on the other side of the car in
back on his as.. impossible to open the door because
I'm so close to the wall I turn around and insult him in
good French he gets up pale and bleeding Usted (he
shouts) iba con luz he goes over and picks up his bicycle and his basket straddles the one and puts the handle
of the other over his arm and goes off leaving tiny little
red drops behind him)

Another car that was following me began to honk and
I saw a furious face in the rearview mirror. I took off
with some anxiety and parked at the harbor. I stepped
over to the wharf, and as I went to light my cigarette I
noticed that my hands were trembling. Five guys had
just come out of the street and were obviously headed
in my direction (I saw them as I went back to examine
the bump on the hood and the left fender of my car).
They were looking at it too, and there was absolutely
no expression on their faces. We just stood there for
quite a long time, until one of them shattered the windshield with the handle of a sturdy knife, then all the
windows, and then two others set about kicking in the
doors; others attacked the lights and the tires and anything else they could find, the whole thing in the most
eerie silence. I stood there watching my car being de-
stroyed, neither doing anything nor saying anything, for
a good while. A crowd had gathered. Behind me I heard
a siren and the motor of a tow car. I finally managed to
take the few strides that separated me from them (that's
what they were waiting for), went up to them, raised my

fists, and got the worst beating of my life. I would never have believed that there could be so many cops in such a small town. They grabbed me, and I didn't need to walk another step. I was struck several times more before finding myself in what was probably a cell, my shoes, my coat, my papers, and my belt (luckily I still had a good tailor in those days) taken away from me. I had been arrested by the enemy authorities, I suppose, on account of that stupid accident, unknown but suspect, not knowing a soul around, and with a guilty conscience. I was then kept under lock and key for a long time. I wanted them to question me, and with this in mind I planned terrific revelations that would not fail to cause talk about me. I could already see that I would then doubtless be executed, a martyr of the Civil War, and perhaps Lucile would shed a few tears over my unfortunate fate. But the only visits I received were the daily ones of a guard with a wooden face that had a mustache running across it, who brought me a bowl of warm soup consisting of bread floating in greasy water, the only nourishment they deigned to give me. He kept to himself and never answered my questions. My prison cell was absolutely empty, with not the least stick of furniture or any conveniences. No light either. The only light I ever saw came from a narrow skylight as high up as a man's head (and with thin bars over it) in the one wall that was made of stone, the three others being simple wooden partitions. As far as I could tell, the skylight overlooked a rather large courtyard, but it was so high up that even if I craned my neck I couldn't see the sky, but only the wall opposite it outside. I wasn't sure how far away this wall was; the distance between me and it even seemed to vary from day to day. One morning I saw that this wall had been covered with a vast network of complicated scaffolding, and then little by little barbed wire began to run the length of the beams, thicker and thicker, like vigorous ivy. Watching this sort of growth, that no worker ever seemed to be working on, was my only pastime until the day that I turned toward the other walls (or partitions). The one on the left was longer (and therefore the one on the right was too, though I did not take the trouble to check this) than the stone wall, and in this left wall was the door through which the guard passed me my food; the one opposite (of the same size, as I have stated) was absolutely bare. But the fourth partition (opposite the skylight) had surprises in store for me. It so happened that either people on the outside who wanted to watch me, or one of my predecessors in this prison, had made a great many tiny holes (fifty-seven in all) in the wood, each around a half-inch in diameter, which I began to use to look out, but only after I had had my fill of the pastime of following the regular trajectory of the luminous pinpoints of light that shone through these holes onto the walls and the ceiling during the day. This was, to be precise, a duty that I imposed upon myself, for I was anxious to keep some occupations in reserve so as to make my stay, which promised to be a long one, more pleasant. Then, experiencing one day an understandable boredom at studying this impalpable escadrille of little points or spots of light that moved imperceptibly, I dashed to the partition and glued my eye to one of the holes. On the first days I saw nothing worth mentioning, even though I spent all my time there. I marked the orifice I had used with a scratch of my fingernail, so as to use one hole a day, and as far as possible never the same one; I saw nothing, it's true, except a greater brightness than that which came through the skylight, and it grew brighter every day, until I finally realized that this partition faced the outside, and that this brightness simply came from the sun. Little by little the scene grew clearer, and I finally was able to make some conjectures about my surroundings. At the beginning all I saw was a stretch of rough cement, but by changing perspective as much as the arrangement permitted, and by persevering, I finally made out the outline of what seemed to be a sort of terrace, bordered by a railing of molded cement (or cut out of wood) that had been painted. In time this terrace came suddenly to have furniture on it, perhaps while I was asleep: iron tables lacquered white, red, and green, and matching chairs, then soon afterward striped umbrellas with advertising slogans in Spanish which I finally managed to decipher: BEBA EL AGUA DE SANTA FE, CERVEZA DEL (the rest invisible, cut off by the perspective), BEBER ES PRECI (likewise), and also a big pennant stretched the whole length of the terrace: ESPAÑA EN PAZ. I realized when the first customers came that the prison had been set up in an inn which was nonetheless still open for business. One day I was awakened by distinct, joyous, somewhat mocking bursts of laughter, and hurrying to my observation post, I saw them: young women for the most part, lightly dressed in colors that were bright but in good taste, with blond hair and tanned shoulders, drinking orange, yellow, and green drinks with a play of sunlight in their translucent depths. They did not say much, but when they did all of them spoke at once, so that I could never make out what their conversations were about. This was the happiest period of my imprisonment. I was very disappointed when the sun grew pale and they got up one by one and left the terrace. I then ate my soup, which had long since grown cold, lay down on the floor, and waited for sleep to come and the sun to bring them back. With the first sounds at dawn, with the first light of day, I was on my feet, my eye glued to the partition. They all looked rather alike and changed their dresses so frequently that I could never make out which was which. This was the way I spent my days, and I would never again have looked in the direction of the skylight if the course of things had not begun to change imperceptibly, and to my misfortune. One fine day I noticed, with both amazement and fear, soon followed by regret, that the pleasure that this spectacle had brought me up to that point was lessening. Each night I tried to think of the possible causes for this change, but could find none, and I almost lost sleep over it. I tried depriving myself of this pastime for several days in a row, with the hope that this boredom was nothing but an illusion brought about by habit, but when I looked out once again, my disappointment went far beyond anything I had imagined. And that's the way it was every day. Their conversations became shrill and embarrassing, as if they were talking about me; their laughter, which was now raucous and grating, seemed to concern me; the umbrellas lost their pretty colors and became so faded and dull that they took them away; the iron of the tables rusted, and the paint cracked and peeled. But I had to bow before an even sadder fact: the women grew older, and from one day to the next grew more careless about their coiffures and even their dress, so quickly that it was terrifying. They even went so far as to behave in a regrettably vulgar manner, farting and scratching themselves shamelessly. I was all the less inclined to observe them in that their stares now seemed to be directed my way every time their laughter got louder, and I then saw these little black eyes draw closer and closer to me, a bit closer all the time, and I was afraid of this stare, till one day I finally gave up what had become more of an obsession than a pastime, knowing that I was in turn being stared at through these holes. I resolutely turned my back on the partition, pretending to ignore it, to forget it, but I nonetheless felt fifty-seven needles stabbing me all the way down my spine. I was immensely relieved when I noticed one morning that they had filled up every last one of the holes with a sort of very resistant cement or putty. My enemies, who doubtless believed that these operations would make me feel bullied or humiliated, didn't know what a favor they'd really done me. At the same time, furthermore, all signs of anybody's presence disappeared from this side of my prison cell. But even this didn't stop me from worrying, for the next morning at the first light of dawn an attempt was made to assassinate me (or to execute me). I say that only after weighing my words. Anybody who knows me knows that, and nothing will lead me to think differently, even if certain people try to prove that what I call an assassination was nothing but an execution in due and proper form, brought about by my crimes, in consequence of a sentence about which I have, I admit, not the slightest personal knowledge. This merely stigmatizes the bad faith and the cowardice of my enemies once more, if there be any need of that. Sooner or later, perhaps thanks to me, the scandalous but beneficent truth will out, the usurpers will be pitilessly cleared out, and this nightmerde will be over. I'm coming to the point. That day, I was awakened early in the morning by subdued metallic sounds coming from the skylight. Without making the slightest gesture, I began to watch the opening, though pretending to be asleep, and I was paying such close attention that I heard the breath of the person who was making the noise I have described. His hands appeared on the sill and gripped the bars, then his face was framed against the dawn light, a young, and even attractive, face, with a strong square chin. Soon I saw his whole torso. He was indeed an elegant man, although he had taken off his

84

suit coat so as to work more comfortably (the work at hand was difficult, certainly), displaying a white shirt with the collar opened slightly underneath an elegant dark-colored silk tie. Without apparent effort, and with just one hand, he yanked off the bars, which had probably been prepared (sawed, for example) to this end without my knowledge. I got up; he gave a terrible smile and brandished his knife. But chance saved me in my panic. I dashed over to the skylight, raised my arms and pushed him, avoiding the knife with a desperate burst of energy, until he let go. Then I saw him literally fly off backward, as if borne by a powerful breeze, and hit the wall opposite, plastered against it, so to speak, and I can still see him there, clinging to the iron beams and the barbed wire like a disjointed scarecrow, his head hanging like a Jesus, and his elegant tie floating in the breeze that sometimes blows. But I don't really think he's dead. They put the bars back up later, and I know that he'll come back, and this next time luck will perhaps be against me. I now spend my days lying staring at the ceiling. For a long time I've been avoiding turning my eyes toward the skylight, except at dawn, and that is the only time of the day that I expect him to return. I've asked Lucile to look; she claims she doesn't see anything, she doesn't believe me, but perhaps they hide when she comes to visit. (I was able to get away because of a bombardment, when the Fascists pounded their own positions. The partitions failed to withstand the first bombs, and I managed to climb along the pillars of the terrace, at the price of terrible wounds. I lived in the woods in the hut of a charcoal-maker, and that is where they picked me up again. They treated me roughly in spite of my infected wounds, and found me another cell, identical to the one before, and the skylight here too overlooks a wall against which my assassin is still plastered, it's still an inn no longer in business, transformed into a war hospital or a prison.) The battles have not stopped, but they are becoming rarer and less violent, timid almost. It's the end. Soon this will be called peace, and the losers will be humiliated, and worse off than before. Spain at peace, an emasculated people. That's why they're keeping me prisoner, under the pretext that they're taking care of me, and because they can't get rid of me. I am one of the last things holding them back, and they have condemned me. But I await my hour as they await theirs. Alone, since for some time Cécile has stopped coming to see me. It seems to me that she used to visit me sometimes, with Coronado, who waited for her outside in their car. He's on the government's side. Last time almost ruined things. They say that I tried to rape her, and that she won't come back. For the present this is doubtless preferable, but we'll always find each other again. They say that I must be patient a while longer, that my wounds are not healed yet. This is true.

3 It was at Aiguesmortes that I took Cécile away from Mathieu. It was a lovely twilight in summer, spoiled by the carnival. When I say that I took her away, this is only a manner of speaking. She was my wife, really my wife I mean, with a civil and religious wedding ceremony and everything (she was a virgin when I took her). But when I say that she was once my wife, that too is only a manner of speaking. The fact that she threw herself into his arms later (after our wedding) merely proves that she was tired of me, not that she loved him, nor that she gave herself to him as completely as she did to me. I haven't really taken her away from him either, because she no longer belonged to anybody. Indifferent, and not knowing herself, any more than anyone else knew her, letting people believe anything, and never saying anything. This was her true face. She was just as she had always been on this fine evening at the end of June.

I was on the ramparts, looking at the canal, which reflected the multicolored lights of the carnival in its shimmering black depths. As I turned back toward the city, I saw her. Astonished to find her alone. I followed them everywhere; he was always with her. I motioned to her, and climbed down. She had put a light blouse on over her bathing suit. Cool colors. She smelled of iodine from the sea. My heart swelled in my breast, as it did every time now. But I couldn't tell her so. She pinched her lips together. Her hair fluttered in the wind. She turned her head away.

I looked too. Mathieu was walking away. Not alone.

"See you in a while," he called.

"Aren't we going to the Casino?" I yelled back.

He didn't answer. Cécile didn't say anything. I watched Mathieu walk away, slim and elegant in his summer outfit, for a moment, then said, turning to her:

"Aren't we going to the Casino?"

"I have no idea."

"Where are they going?"

"I have no idea. To have an apéritif."

"How about us? You and me, I mean?"

"I'm hungry already. Take me to supper, if you like."

"What about him?"

"He'll find us."

We were driving toward the harbor. She was driving.

"This convertible of yours is nice," she said.

"It's a bachelor's car," I observed.

On the terrace we ate shellfish and a fine bouillabaisse. The white wine was cool and dry. She talked to me about the bullfights that they had seen at Arles the week before, before I arrived.

"I'd like to sleep with you," I said.

"Me too," she said.

"Does Mathieu make love well?"

"No, not well."

"Well then?"

"No."

We went to have a few Scotches at the harbor and watched the light in the lighthouse revolve.

"Let's go back," she said. "Drive me."

I tried to be gallant: opening the car door and so forth.

"You still drive just as badly as ever."

"I was thinking about something else."

"Liar."

"I'm not lying. I was thinking about you."

"Of course. You don't need to think to do that."

"I like what you're saying. That's true."

I watched her push back the lock of hair that had fallen over her forehead.

"Look at the road."

"I'm looking at you."

"That's all right with me."

"It's not all right with me. But I have to look at you."

"Stop."

I parked the car on the shoulder of the road. I had to get out first. She got out on the same side because of the ditch, and took a few steps on the pink asphalt in her bare feet, not saying a word.

"Mathieu didn't join us," I said.

"He didn't say he would."

"Why did you marry him?"

"Because he asked me to."

"There's no hope for me?"

"I'll let you hope whatever you like. It doesn't interest me. I'm warning you, the way you're acting exasperates me. Talk about something else for a little while."

"I can't."

"Let's go back then."

She was getting away from me. Even though I had once been able to bend her to my will to the point that I got tired of her. As strong now against me as she had once been weak with me. I was suffering from her (relative) beauty.

"Take me to the circus," she said.

"It's not a circus," I said. "There's no circus. It's some itinerant boxers."

"That doesn't matter. I want to go. I've never seen any boxing."

She had certainly not grown any uglier. On the contrary. I must be the one who made her ugly, or else the one who ended up finding her so. In any case, it wasn't Mathieu who made her look pretty. But rather the distance, the absence (between her and me). I told her so.

We left the car under the ramparts. I bought her some candy, and we rode big pink wooden pigs, and soon we were both on the same one. Me behind. I put my arm around her waist, caressing her under her breast. She was having as good a time as a little girl. She turned around and laughed.

"You look silly," she said. "Let go of me."

"Louder," I said. "I can't hear over the music."

She leaned back and said in my ear, very low but distinctly: "You're stupid."

I thought I could take the liberty of hugging her tighter. But the merry-go-round soon stopped.

"Another ride?"

"No let's go to the circus instead."

"It's not a circus."

I helped her jump off. Mathieu must have been standing there watching us for a moment. He was pale. It didn't go well with his light clothes. The woman who had been with him had disappeared. Cécile asked:

"Where were you?"

"I had an apéritif."

"Did you have dinner?"

"I will in a while," he said. "I'm not hungry right now. How about you?"

"We ate at the Grau at the harbor."

"Oh, good. What's happening now?"

"We're going to the circus," I said.

"It's not a circus," he explained. "There's a dancer and some boxers."

We moved on finally. He put his arm around her waist.

"Who with?"

"Some friends. Aren't you going to ask about the bet I made?"

"No. What friends?"

"I made a bet, you know," he said. "I bet that I would go box with their champ. I was at their parade a while ago and at the show afterward. It's rather fun. You can even win five thousand francs."

"I think that's idiotic," she said.

"Let's go," I said.

"I signed up with the boss. They've got a Negro boxer."

"Shut up. Kiss me."

"I had to have a couple of drinks to get used to the idea."

"Shut up, will you?"

I was walking a little way behind them. He was thin and nervous, and not without charm. He had his arm around her waist, as I've said. She was walking gracefully along, little and thin, and I admired her tan. Her blond hair was floating on her copper-colored neck. I would have liked to say something. But she had forgotten me. Mathieu expressed a desire to have a beer at the drink stand.

It was still warm out. He was the only one thinking about his fight. He left us in front of the tent. I got two tickets and stood aside for Cécile to go ahead. There were lots of people and lots of noise. We settled down in the seats as best we could, with the knees of the people behind us in our backs. I could feel her thigh against mine. I passed my arm around behind her, and at first rested it on the iron bar we were leaning against. Her thigh was warm, and her thin dress betrayed her every shiver. But she wasn't shivering, just moving restlessly about.

"Why is Mathieu doing this?" I asked. "What's he trying to prove?"

"Nothing. He just wants to have fun."

"That isn't any fun."

"Be quiet and watch."

There was a bad dancer, more or less of an acrobat, but all the same it was a woman's body, almost nude beneath the sequins. The excited crowd was only mildly interested in her act. Cécile was nibbling away at a bar of nougat. She stuck a piece of it in my mouth, laughing. I don't like nougat, even if it's from Montélimar.

A boxing exhibition came next. Then it was Mathieu's turn. He appeared, in good trim, his torso naked, but the giant-sized boxing gloves hanging from the end of his arms made his nervous shoulders look thin. Mathieu was clumsy and aggressive. The Negro boxer kept maneuvering him though. Mathieu doubtless realized this and began to hit out in a rage. Cécile bit her lips. The Negro got mad, and began to give Mathieu what was coming to him. Soon I was suffering for him: his eye was black, his lip split and swollen. The fight went on.

"Let's go," Cécile said.

She got up. The fight was still going on. The spectators were stamping and whistling.

"What about Mathieu?" I asked.

"Stay if you like."

I got up too and followed her. Mathieu was huddled on a stool and seemed to be looking in our direction with his one good eye. There was still one round left.

"Let's get out of this racket," she said when we got outside.

I took her by the arm for fear that we'd be separated by the crowd.

"Aren't we going to wait for him?"

"He'll go have dinner. I don't want to eat dinner twice."

We walked to the ramparts. The carnival lights went out for the fireworks display. We watched it from the top of the patrol road. There was lots of noise. I looked at Cécile's face, raised toward the moving sky.

"How can he leave you?" I said. "I was always tagging after you."

"You haven't changed," she said without looking at me.

"No. He's not like me."

"He's very jealous," she said.

"I am too," I said.

"Stop it."

She shivered. I put my arm around her shoulders.

"Are you cold?"

"Yes. Let's go down to the town. I want to go back. No, not in the car."

I decided not to say anything more. But everything in me was an appeal, as everything in her was doubtless a refusal. As we walked along, I looked at her often. I was saying to myself: Cécile—Cécile—Cécile. We were now in the narrow alleyways. The houses here are very old and delightful. But we knew all that by heart. Mathieu too.

"You can't drive through here in a car," I said. "In the morning there are donkeys carrying baskets to the market."

Suddenly she pressed close to me.

"What are you doing here with me?" she asked.

I stared at the ground without answering. And we slowed down. I caressed the hollow of her thigh, with longer and longer strokes, going up almost to her armpit, which was warm and just a bit damp. Then I brought my hand up to my nostrils, breathing in this pure feminine odor.

"I'd like to find you again," I finally said.

"You're looking in the wrong place," she said.

"But you know that I'm looking for you. Answer me this time."

She said nothing. She was completely passive. I pulled

her gently by one arm. She followed me to my hotel under the arcades of the plaza. I can't remember the name of this plaza. I only know that it reminds me of Saint Louis. It was cooler now. We drank a Scotch at the bar and she began to talk of their vacation. They were planning to leave for Spain at the beginning of the week. She talked a great deal. Suddenly she stopped, and then went on:

"I hope you aren't listening to me."

"I'm looking at you," I said.

"That's all you know how to do."

I got up first, and took her arm. I asked the desk clerk for the key and we went upstairs. I would have liked to look at her (rediscover her) but she immediately got undressed. She stretched out on the bed and asked me for a cigarette, which she puffed on just once before putting it out. I sat down on the edge of the bed. Her belly was delicately curved. I put my hand on it, and then my mouth. She sighed, as if she were annoyed.

We must both have disappointed each other. I remember that I was disappointed. We fell asleep, and it was she who woke me in the night. Without being gentle about it. To tell me that she had been watching me sleep. The moonlight showed me her face, with a beautiful play of shadow. She kissed me on the neck (spontaneously). Her nose was cold. This time I was happy when I fell asleep.

I awoke long before she did. It was already broad daylight. You could hear the noises and shouts of the market. Cécile was still there, naked and warm. Silky. The first time in four years. I raised the sheet and she whimpered softly. She seemed very close again. As she had been in the past. I forced myself not to think about it at all.

"I was pretending to be asleep," she said.

"Why?"

"No reason. I don't want to go back with you."

"Why?"

"Stop always asking the same questions. First of all, because I'm married."

"That didn't keep you from leaving me," I said.

"No, but it's different this time."

"Because of Mathieu?"

"It's not because I'm here, because I'm sleeping in your bed, that I came back."

"How everything has changed," I said.

"You're the one who's changed."

"No, you're the one."

She took a bath while I shaved. Then we went downstairs to breakfast. She didn't want me to take her back to where she was staying. I went for a walk through the market. I looked at the women. All the women, counting those I would have liked to make love with. I counted twelve, and stopped counting. I bought a wicker basket, some red burgundy and some white, some cold beef and some shellfish. I went to get my car, put everything on the back seat, and slowly headed for Boucanet beach. I sought out a quiet spot. There were plenty of them. I swam, had lunch, and slept. I felt fine.

I happened to go by their hotel that evening. They were loading suitcases into their sedan. Cécile was licking an ice-cream cone.

"Are you leaving?" I said.

"Apparently," Mathieu said. "We're going to Spain. If you feel like it . . . " he added, no longer looking at me.

"I don't see any reason why he should change his vacation plans," Cécile interrupted.

"I don't either," I said, without thinking one way or the other.

"It's not important," Mathieu said.

His eye and his lips were still swollen. He got behind the wheel. Cécile was humming a catchy tune and doing a dance step on the sidewalk. Mathieu started the motor, took time out to light a cigarette, and shot off.

"He's crazy," I said. "Where's he going?"

"He'll be back," she said calmly, throwing away her cone. "Buy me a drink."

We sat down on the terrace and drank pastis. I asked for some crackers and anchovies, shrimps, and olives. Mathieu wasn't back.

"He's not jealous," I said point-blank.

"Yes, he is. You get on my nerves. He might kill you. Even if you didn't deserve it."

I paid no more attention to her. I looked at my watch. He'd been gone half an hour.

"What's he up to?" I finally said.

"I have no idea. Maybe he's had an accident."

"Let's go see."

"Where?"

"He certainly didn't go toward the ocean. It's a dead end that way."

"So?"

"We'll ask at the service station."

Mathieu had filled the tank as he passed by, before taking the main highway that goes back north.

"Don't drive so fast," Cécile said.

I felt guilty. I had known Mathieu for ten years when he introduced me to Cécile at the University. I was playing out a little inner melodrama, chewing over the fact that our adolescence was really more of a common bond between us than the fact that we'd loved the same woman.

"Stop," Cécile said.

Mathieu's car was half hidden in a ditch. You could see the whole bottom of the rear; it looked as if the car had flipped over. He wasn't far off. On the other side of the road. He was holding a man in a sitting position. We went over. There was blood everywhere. There was a strong smell: warm blood, and burned rubber too.

"What did you do?" Cécile asked.

He looked at us without answering. He looked terribly unhappy, and his handsome shirt was spotted with blood. The man he was holding up was hiccuping gently. He was cut terribly about the face, and seemed to be disjointed. His head was flopped pitifully over onto his chest, as if his neck were broken. I bent over and brushed Mathieu's shoulder lightly.

"You shouldn't touch people who have been hurt," I said softly.

"Don't just stand there," Cécile cried in exasperation.

I left them and went to telephone for the ambulance. The three of us spent the night in the hospital grounds. The surgeon and the nurse sent us packing when we asked for news. Around four o'clock they told us he wasn't too bad, but that at best he would probably be crippled and seriously handicapped. He had a family. Stupid things like that happen.

"You're even stupider than that," Cécile said.

I drove them to the station. The hot wind from the south was no longer blowing. It looked gray out. Mathieu fell into a stubborn silence, staring into space. Cécile's hair was all mussed up, and her set little face looked worn after a night without sleep. She looked chilled and sickly, her head hunched down into her shoulders. As Mathieu climbed up onto the step of the train, I said to him:

"Don't worry."

"Damn," he replied.

Back in Paris, some time went by without our seeing each other. Then I ran into them several times, at the theater and at concerts. They invited me to bridge parties. All this became a habit: theater, concerts, bridge. Mathieu often watched me. Cécile ignored me. These weren't exactly planned meetings, but almost. They always told me where they were planning to go, and seemed to be disappointed when something kept me away or a sudden whim* dictated that I go elsewhere. They were both bored, bored with each other. I was sure of it.

They perhaps needed the threat of my presence, or the vivid memories that my presence revived, to find each other again. She seemed more and more beautiful to me. But he, on the other hand, seemed to be withering away. Not that he neglected his appearance, for his clothes were still elegant, but his skin looked gray. Cécile told me one day that the *lycée* bored him and tired him.

This lasted two or three months perhaps, until the evening that I found Cécile alone on the Place des Ternes. It was raining. She was wearing a very handsome light raincoat. No purse. She was pacing back and forth, her hands in her pockets, looking charming even so.

"Where's Mathieu?" I asked.

"I don't know," she said. "He was supposed to meet me at home the day before yesterday after his classes. I waited till the last minute for him tonight. You're late."

"What'll we do?"

"Go anyway. Outside of the rhapsodies you don't get to hear Bartok every day." *

It was a very pleasant evening. The music made her

---

* He doesn't have any.
* Vive Bartok.

happy. I asked her if she was trying not to appear concerned. She said not. During the intermission we consulted a weekly entertainment program and decided where we'd go next. I didn't ask any questions about Mathieu. I even managed to be prudent enough not to annoy her. We'll go here, we'll go there, that was all. She was in a good mood. We had owned some Bartok records in common. I asked her about them, as if it were an offhand question. She still listened to them.

"They're out of date technically," I said.

"I don't notice it. You made good choices."

I went with her as far as her street. She rang and disappeared behind the heavy porte-cochere. I listened to her footfalls: growing fainter in the vestibule, bumping against the first steps, dying away. I was waiting for a light to appear at the front of the building. She turned a light on. Instead of getting back into my car, I walked to the corner café-tobacco shop and went in. I ordered a snack and some beer, grabbed a newspaper lying around on one of the benches, and managed to while away an hour.

"I'm closing up," the waiter said.

"O.K. May I use the telephone?"

I dialed Cécile's number. It rang five or six times before someone picked up the receiver.

"Hello," a sleepy voice said.

"Is that you, Cécile?"

"Who'd you think it would be?" she said in an annoyed voice.

"Were you sleeping?"

"I'm not any more."

"Are you alone?"

"You know very well that I am."

"If I had known, I wouldn't have left."

"I don't need anybody."

"I need you."

". . ."

"Listen, can I come up?"

"If you want to, but I don't see any necessity for it."

She hung up. So much the better. I went right over. She hadn't drawn the bolt on the front door. But she had gotten out of bed and put on pretty mules to receive me.

"What's the use of coming back?" she said. "We were getting along very well a while ago (pretty well)."

"That's right," I said. "That was perhaps the first time."

"If you don't have anything to say, I'm going back to sleep."

"I'll wait for you."

She went back to bed and closed her eyes. I turned out the light and settled down in an armchair. I listened to her breathing: it was regular. She was fast asleep. A half-hour later she stirred and turned over with a soft moan. I watched her there in the dark out of the corner of my eye. She propped herself up on one elbow, and it was she who called me. I didn't answer, and gave a deep sigh. She got up then. I saw her come right up next to me, and I felt her breath, already a bit stale from sleeping.

"Don't stay here," she said. "Come on."

It was warm where she'd been sleeping. Soon it was an oven. This time I felt that she was getting pleasure from it. (She had not done so at Aiguesmortes.) We woke up in each other's arms, cramped and with pins and needles in our arms and legs. She moved in with me that very night. She did the cooking, and moved the furniture about. She brought along her records and her stuffed animals.

At the beginning I didn't work much; most of my time

was devoted to her. But soon we settled down and I found her less beautiful, that is to say less desirable. Her personality irritated me. I asked her to get a divorce and marry me again. She told me that the idea was amusing, that people in America often did that, but she didn't answer my question.

She wasn't enough for me, but I needed her. Doubtless she knew this. That is why she said nothing, leaving me up in the air. One night when I came home from my office, I found the house empty. It was really empty. A plush rabbit was perched on the coffee table where the telephone was. I called Mathieu's, and then her mother's. No news.

It was she who called me the next day at my office.

"Where were you?" I asked.

"Home."

"What do you mean, *home*?"

"At my place. I went over to get the mail and stayed over to sleep."

"You might have told me first. I was very worried."

"Can you meet me?"

"Of course."

She gave me the address of a café.

"I've had a letter from Mathieu," she told me when she got there.

"What's become of him? What does he have to say?"

"That he's better. He asks us to forgive his running away. No, he doesn't really ask us to forgive him. He just says he couldn't help it. That . . . He's in a rest home in the mountains. I think he mentioned it to me once. It must be a rest home for teachers."

"He must have been suffering from asthenia," I ventured.

"He's not suffering from anything at all. I'd like to have a clear conscience on that score."

She said no more. I remarked shortly that it had been raining steadily ever since Mathieu left. I looked vaguely at the gates of the town hall, on the other side of the square.

"Why don't we get married again?" I asked bluntly.

"We'll talk about that later," she said.

I put my arm around her waist.

"He gave me his address," she said. "We ought to go see him. But if you don't want to go with me, I'll go alone."

"I have no claims on you," I said.

"I'd like it better if you'd come with me. Might as well get everything settled once and for all."

I didn't quite know what she meant. But I was happy to find her again, for to tell the truth I'd had a good scare. Moreover, she apparently was trying to be nice.

"When shall we go?" I asked.

"As soon as you can."

"I can get off whenever I want to," I assured her.

"Let's wait till tomorrow. Or even a few days more. We can go to the movies tonight. I feel like going to a movie. Will you take me out to eat?"

And she gave me a light little kiss.

We found a nice inn six miles or so from the rest home where Mathieu had chosen to stay. We were on the side of a hill, not far from a river whose name escapes me. The place was deserted, and as wild as anyone could have wished. Unfortunately, the food was mediocre. She had asked for separate rooms, but this wasn't hard to get around; we were the only clients, and what few hotel servants there were were discreet. In a word, winter there was not without its charms.*

---

* That's what you think.

102

We spent the first week taking rides around the countryside. Cécile liked the medieval ruins. She would spend hours pacing up and down in the courtyard of old châteaux, grubbing in the stones, tirelessly contemplating crumbled coats of arms. The air was bracing, and she looked splendid.

We hadn't talked about Mathieu yet. I decided to let her take the lead. One morning she said to me:

"I'm going to see Mathieu today."

"Certainly," I said.

"If you want to come along, you can wait for me at the door. That would be better this first time," she added.

"I doubt that he's very sick," I said. "We'll have to have a talk with him soon. If you don't, I will."

"Are you really that anxious?" she inquired.

"Yes, I am. I want to marry you."

"Well, in that case, you take care of things. . . . Maybe you won't though. If you do, you'll have wanted all the rest, I mean everything that could happen afterward. Whether you speak to him or not is not a matter of indifference to me," she added with a smile.

I took her there in the car. She stayed barely an hour. She came back with her hair mussed and looking a little pale.

"He brought it up first," she said immediately. "He doesn't want a divorce. I know him. He'll hold out."

"How is he?"

"Pretty good. He looks better. The service is marvelous. The place must cost a lot. He shouldn't stay there anyway. He's not sick. It's as if he were in hiding. He absolutely must leave. I asked to talk to the director, who's also the head doctor around the place. He'll see us tomorrow."

The director's broad smile, his impeccable teeth, and his gold-rimmed glasses inspired confidence. He asked us to sit down and talked to us about Mathieu for quite a while. We sat there like grade-school pupils in front of their teacher.

"Your husband, dear madame," he said, "doesn't belong here. For one thing, this is a private institution, and therefore expensive, and moreover most of our patients are mental cases. Here he's in the company of people who in the long run may possibly have a bad influence on him. He's not sick; what he needs most of all is fresh air and rest. The school authorities could get this for him at a much cheaper rate, and furthermore they have special facilities."

"Did you say that he really isn't sick?"

"Absolutely."

He smiled.

"He's obviously a bit anxiety-ridden. He's a sort of (he waved his hands as he spoke) neurotic labor leader, suffering from a slight guilt complex, with just a touch of sexual obsession. He doubtless tends a bit toward self-analysis, or self-pity if you prefer. But that's all quite normal in a man as overworked as he obviously is. This is frequently the case with intellectuals."

He spoke like doctors in publicity shorts at the movies advertising toothpaste (or some other product). In any case, what he said seemed frank and to the point.

"It's a crisis," he said, "that only time can cure. I suppose you understand what I mean," he added. "Obviously it's going to take a lot of your time."

Since he seemed to be addressing me, I nodded my head.

In the car, Cécile took me into her confidence:

"I'd like to be sure that they aren't throwing him out because he chased the nurses. Does that amuse you?"

"That's stupid," I said. "They're used to it. What they're really afraid of is that he won't be able to afford a long treatment."

Two days later Cécile left alone in my convertible to go get Mathieu. When I saw them come back, I shut myself up in my bedroom and picked up a newspaper. I felt a little nervous. They both invaded my room, and Cécile kept bursting into laughter. He looked fine, in spite of his dirty, worn clothes. There was something secretly distinguished about him, as usual; that was the source of his strength, of his superiority over me. Something childlike, perhaps, that I didn't have.

"How are you?" he asked.

"I should be asking you that," I said as I got up.

"Just look at me. Cécile seems to be in good shape too."

She was hanging back in the shadow of the corridor.

"You should take a bath," she said. "Tomorrow we'll go into town to buy you a suit."

"Right. Will you go with us?"

"Absolutely not," I said.

"She won't be able to get along without you," he said, looking out of the window. "She told me so herself. What a fine view."

He turned around so abruptly that I gave a start despite myself.

"Did you sleep in your room or in Cécile's?"

"That depended," Cécile said dryly. "But the view from here is better."

"Things will be more complicated now that I'm here."

He seemed to be extraordinarily self-possessed. I made up my mind to smile; I would gain nothing by being hostile. And I could lose everything as far as Cécile was concerned.

We went down to dinner. As we went past the hotel manager, he said to him:

"Naturally there's no need to reserve a room for me. I intend to stay only a short time, and I'll use Madame's room, since it looks as if there's room enough."

"Very well, monsieur."

We didn't say a word during dinner. That is to say, Cécile and I didn't say a word. He was amused by this, and his nonchalance came as a surprise. It finally got on his nerves, but we forced ourselves to pay no attention to the sly digs he kept making.

He suggested a game of bridge, and invited the hotel manager to play. I beat him twice, once with Cécile, and then with the manager.

"Luck's with the traveling salesman tonight," Mathieu said.

I said nothing.

"Everybody knows," he announced, "that even though traveling salesmen lead a gay life, they all have horns."

"That reminds me," I said, "I have to do something for the southeast branch. The president and chairman of the board wants to buy a warehouse. Will you come with me?"

"Not me," Cécile said drily. "I'm tired."

"Certainly," Mathieu said. "I've been weaned away from walks for quite a while now. It'll give me a chance to try my hand at driving again."

"Right."

Cécile got up, and put her hands on Mathieu's shoulders. I felt a hot flush creep over me.

"Let's go up to bed," she said. "I'm exhausted."

They left the room. The manager had discreetly disappeared. In one hour I absorbed the contents of a bottle half full of cognac that was sitting on the bridge table. I took two aspirins with the last glass.* I went to my room, trying not to make any noise. I undressed, went to bed, and was soon sound asleep.

I hadn't closed the door. Mathieu came in and plunked down on the bed. I opened my eyes painfully and groped about for the switch to the lamp on the night table.

"No use putting the light on," he said. "Cigarette?"

"Thanks. What do you want?"

"Nothing. Cécile's left."

"Left? What do you mean?"

"On the train. She called a taxi."

I sat up, wide awake.

"How long has she been gone?"

"A good hour."

He was in his shirt sleeves. I saw him moving about in the dark.

"There wasn't anything I could do."

"You should have come and gotten me."

"It wouldn't have mattered. In any case, she didn't leave anything behind for you."

"Ass."

I was beside myself. I got up, got dressed, stuck my head under the faucet. I turned on all the lights.

"What are you doing? She's already on the train."

"I can get to the Gare de Lyon before she does."

"That'd surprise me, what with all the ice. You couldn't catch her even if the road was in good condition."

"You're right. But I'm leaving anyway."

"You can wait till tomorrow. I have to talk to you."

I sat down again.

"Go ahead," I said.

"Turn off all these lights, good Christ. Have you got anything to drink?"

---

* In their room, however, M. and C. were probably making love.

"On the dresser."

"Good. That's better. So you want to know why she left. Because of me. I disappointed her. I wanted to make love with her, and I couldn't. I'm impotent. It's my new disease."

"I don't give a damn."

"That's the only reason, you understand."

"Will you shut up?"

"Don't yell so loud," he said. "You can imagine what a hassle it was. Then she got annoyed and got up and left. Maybe she's with the stationmaster," he smirked. "You might tell me that I'm her husband, that it's not all that serious, that the bitch will be back. But you know very well that you're never really married to her. She's, how shall I put it, much more a fiancée and a mistress than she is a wife."

He knew her well. He exasperated me. I had an unbearable headache, and I was vainly racking my brains for a way to catch her.

"If you want to see her again," he said, "I advise you to wait a few days. But it won't get you anywhere. I won't divorce her in any event. I'll keep her that way. I'll keep her in any case. Just because she sleeps with you here and there. . . . My lord, what a little slut. However, all I had to do was appear on the scene, like tonight, and the other day at the asylum."

"She's a little slut all right."

"She had. . . . She had everything to make her a wife worthy of the name. Listen, *you* know what that tender flesh was like. I got the goods when she was a virgin."

"All right," I said. "I've let you run on for a while, that's enough, will you shut up!"

"Don't yell."

"Do you want me to punch you one?"

He brought his hand up to his ear.

"Of course not, calm down. I'm more to be pitied than you are. What's left of me? In fact, what's left of us? Of you and her? Bidet stories. Of me and her? Nothing. Defeat. Of the two of us, you and me? Of ten years of being friends, maybe more, of dreams we shared?"

"You trying to make me burst into tears?"

"We don't have anything. Neither her, nor you, nor me. Everybody's out for number one, everybody talks only about himself, and nobody's got anybody."

He began swinging his feet over the edge of the bed. It was four o'clock in the morning.

"Is our trip tomorrow still on?"

"More than ever," I said.

The idiot finally went to sleep. I saw his profile gleaming in the moonlight. He looked absolutely innocent. I had punched him just once, a long time ago. He was big enough to look after himself. He hadn't said a word.

He was asleep.

I curled up at the end of the bed and went to sleep too.

It was he who woke me up. It was already daylight, but it had doubtless not been light long. He was already dressed and freshly shaved.

"Come on," he said. "The manager has gotten us something to eat."

We picked at our breakfast.

"Shall I drive?"

"If you like," I said.

As the car took off, a noise made me turn around, and I saw one of the balcony windows open. And Cécile shouted at us:

"Be careful."

With a friendly wave.

"You see," he said, raising his voice because of the

wind and the noise of the motor, "she didn't leave. And I have a good hard on."

He burst out laughing.

"Let go of me, you're going to crack us both up. Don't be an idiot."

He got right down to the heart of the matter:

"I should have let you go. I wanted you to go. Then I changed my mind. I thought we could talk together. It's better that you stayed. It's more honest. Shall I take the main highway?"

I nodded. I'd been had. Yes and no. Better not to get back on the subject. He drove fast and well. He hadn't stopped smiling. After about twelve miles on the main highway, I had him cross the Rhone.

"Turn left," I said to him then.

A very narrow road climbed gently up to an immense iron and wood building with broken windowpanes. It smelled of cold, damp earth.

"It's over there," I said.

He parked the car next to the wall and turned the motor off. There wasn't a sound now.

"Do you have a key?"

"No need for one. It's open; nobody's interested in it. That's why it's a good buy. Come on."

The soil was rich and the grass was wet. We entered the building. There was a large empty room and all around the top of it a complicated arrangement of wooden partitions, stairways, shaky passageways, and iron ladders.

"You go first," I said.

"You're the owner."

"Not yet."

"What are you going to do here?"

"Store things packed in cardboard cartons."

"It seems very damp to me."

"Maybe so, but you don't know anything about it. Let's go up there on the right."

We got almost to the top and stopped in a passageway of thin boards that ran the length of the room, underneath the windows. He leaned over the railing.

"It's high," he commented.

"About four stories high," I said.

"Good Christ."

He was pale. His heart must have been beating as mine was, in deep surges that could be felt all the way up to the throat.

"You know," he said without looking at me, "Cécile really did leave, but . . . but she couldn't get a train, so she came back. And this time we did make love. She's the one who told me to come here with you."

"Some more of your bullshit."

"No, it's not. She wanted to go find you, the little slut. I told her you'd cut out."

"What? What about my car?"

"She didn't bother to check."

"The bitch."

"What makes you say that? She's my wife."

He was paler still now. He was toying with an iron bar that had been standing against the wall a moment before. I took a step toward him. His shoulders hunched over.

"She's not worth what you're trying to do," he said. "And I warn you that I'm going to defend myself."

No, she really wasn't worth what I was trying to do. I came forward nonetheless. The iron bar just grazed me. I threw myself on him, crouching down low, and hung on to him as hard as I could. As I had a firm grip on him, he let go of his improvised weapon. He began to push me hard, I was stronger than he was, I should have been able to resist, but soon I felt the railing crushing

111

my vertebrae. He bore down on me with all his weight, bending me double over the railing, and I realized that he was deliberately trying to strangle me. My back began to pain me and I couldn't straighten up. Then suddenly something cracked and gave way behind me, and I was sure that everything was giving way, the balustrade, the partitions, the ladders, and the roof along with all the rest, as we fell, still clutching each other, down through a deafening racket, which sounded like a tremendous clash of cymbals.

It was a long night for me, punctuated by gleaming flashes of lightning and enormous rumbles which distended my body. When it was over, it was already June, I remember very well that it was a beautiful afternoon in June, and this is the only memory I have of that time that is not comatose. People had already spoken to me about it, quite often, but I was still in a sort of half sleep. They had told me that I needed rest, that it wasn't really amnesia, that everything would come back to me, but I didn't want it to come back, and I told the story of my life, living and reliving it as if in a dream, docile and a bit dazed. There was, however, some reason to be concerned, for I must have been subject to vertigo even before my accident. I should have been more careful. I also had to see my lawyer, for my wife had instituted divorce proceedings. I refused to see him. But as I was saying, it was on this afternoon in the middle of June that I really woke up. There's a pretty young woman who wants to see you, the nurse tells me. I'm going to go with you.

She helped me out of bed. I felt fine. She guided me out of my room gently, holding me by the arm, and took me into a vast, completely bare corridor. I felt really fine. "The (she said) visiting room is at the other end of the corridor we'll come and get you."

So I waited.

112